"We'd drive each other crazy if we pretended to be married."

"Most likely, yes," Sam said. "But we could always try it out and see."

Kim decided to play along with him for a bit. "It might cramp your style," she said, levelly. "As a wife, I won't tolerate you gallivanting around with other women."

His mouth twitched. "I don't gallivant. And what about you? Would it cramp *your* style?"

Kim waved her hand. "I'm off men. Okay," she said. "I'll be your wife."

Ever since **Karen van der Zee** was a child growing up in Holland she wanted to do two things: write books and travel. She's been very lucky. Her American husband's work as a development economist has taken them to many exotic locations. They were married in Kenya, had their first daughter in Ghana and their second in the United States. They spent two fascinating years in Indonesia. Since then they've added a son to the family and lived for a number of years in Virginia before going on the move again. After spending over a year in the West Bank near Jerusalem and three and a half years in Ghana (again), they are now living in Armenia, but not for good!

HIRED WIFE

KAREN VAN DER ZEE

THE MARRIAGE QUEST

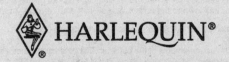

HARLEQUIN®

TORONTO • NEW YORK • LONDON
AMSTERDAM • PARIS • SYDNEY • HAMBURG
STOCKHOLM • ATHENS • TOKYO • MILAN • MADRID
PRAGUE • WARSAW • BUDAPEST • AUCKLAND

ISBN 0-373-80630-2

HIRED WIFE

First North American Publication 2000.

Copyright © 1999 by Karen van der Zee.

CHAPTER ONE

THE BEDROOM door creaked softly and Kim stirred in the big bed. Through half-opened eyes she saw the man enter—a dark, floating shape in the moon-shadowed room, mysterious, undefined. Outside the open window, palm fronds rustled in the cool sea breeze and she could hear the gentle rushing of the waves lapping onto the beach.

The door closed behind him and he moved toward the bed, soundlessly. She caught a glimmer of white, a dress shirt? Slowly she began to see more. He was tall and she could see the outline of strong, square shoulders. His face was in darkness. She willed her eyes to see, to focus. She noticed the movements of his arms and hands as he unbuttoned his shirt and pulled it off. The moonlight silvered over his broad, bare chest.

She could not see his face.

It did not matter. She closed her eyes, waiting, smiling in the dark, wondering where she was. An island?

The breeze floated over the bed, stroking her face, and naked shoulders, carrying the scents of sea and sand and some exotic night-flowering bloom. The sheets were cool against her skin. A slow, languorous sigh escaped her. She felt blissful, sleepy soft, the beginnings of a delicious warmth stirring in her blood.

Waiting, wanting, drifting.

She felt him beside her, felt his body against hers, warm and hard and strong. He put his arms around her and she nestled into his embrace. He was so big and she was so small; he nearly swallowed her.

Happiness suffused her. She belonged in these arms,

5

sheltered, safe. At the center of her, desire stirred. The
scent of him filled her and her blood began to tingle
through her body as if it were champagne.

"Hello, Kim," he whispered near her ear.

"Hi," she whispered back, heady with his nearness.

He began to kiss her, tender kisses by her right ear,
her temple, her closed eyes, her cheek. He had reached
her mouth. "You smell delicious," he murmured against
her lips, his voice deep, intoxicating.

His hands joined in the caressing and her body sang
with his touch. A yearning, deep and real, captured her
heart and soul and body—a yearning to love him, this
man in her bed, to hold him and cherish him and never
let him go.

He whispered something magical and secret she did
not understand.

She looked up at his face. It was still hidden in the
darkness. Reaching up, she traced her fingers along his
hard square jaw, newly shaven, and along his cheeks and
nose and wide forehead—a strong, manly face, she
knew. She touched her fingertips to his mouth.

"Who are you?" she whispered.

Floating out of darkness into light, bright light, Kim
moaned in protest. She wanted to slip back into the vel-
vety darkness, a darkness full of sensuous delights and
pleasures.

The sounds of New York City traffic, muffled, familiar, insinuated themselves into her consciousness. She
buried her face in the pillow. She wanted the sounds of
the waves washing ashore, the sound of whispered words
of love, the exquisite sensation of his hands stroking her
body. Slowly she inhaled the air, her eyes closed, willing
herself to smell the sea breeze, the scent of the man who
shared her bed. Nothing.

Surfacing. She struggled against it, not wanting to

leave behind the magic of the night, but knowing she had to.

A police car, the siren going full blast, shrieked down a nearby street, shredding the last of the veil of sleep. Kim sighed. There was no denying it; she was awake, totally completely awake. And sadly aware of the cold reality that there had been no lover in her bed last night.

It was the third time in two weeks that she'd had the dream. It was a wonderful dream, no question, but what was the meaning of it? Who was the man? It was a tad disturbing, really, making love with a man she didn't know. Shame on her! Still, in some mysterious way he seemed familiar, as if she knew him somehow.

She hoisted herself up into a sitting position and with both hands wiped the hair out of her face, over her shoulders. It was a mess; she couldn't even get her fingers through it.

It didn't make sense for her to be having a dream like this, especially now. She was fed up with men, at least for the moment.

For a while she wanted no more love and romance to complicate her life. Men demanded so much attention and coddling and ego-stroking; she really was quite tired of it and felt in need of a well-deserved man rest. Now if only Tony would quit bothering her she might find a little peace.

She'd met him at a party three weeks ago, and it hadn't taken long to realize that the only topic of conversation of interest to Tony, was Tony. Much to her despair, he had taken an immediate fancy to her and was now making a nuisance of himself by devising various crazy schemes to gain her interest.

She was not interested.

Amused, maybe, but not interested. He did have a sense of humor, she had to give him that. She swung her legs over the edge of the bed and grinned, thinking

of the hideous painting of a half-dead weeping willow
he'd sent her as a joke two days ago, accompanied by a
poem—something impressively maudlin about how he
wept like the willow for being unable to gain her love.
Last week he'd sent her reservations on a love boat
cruise through the Caribbean. She'd returned them, of
course—not that she didn't want to go on a cruise, but
she wasn't for sale.

Cruise. Islands. Palm trees. She was thinking about
the unknown lover in her bed again, the feel of his naked
body against hers. She groaned. *Stop it,* she told herself.
Stop it! She struggled to her feet, swaying a little, feeling
a distinct lack of energy. The dream sure had taken it
out of her.

In the bathroom she turned on the shower and gingerly
tested the temperature of the water. Jason, who shared
her spacious loft apartment with her, liked his water frig-
idly cold—some torturous regimen to keep him awake
so he could work on his doctoral dissertation, something
excruciatingly brainy to do with statistics. She adjusted
the temperature and stepped into the warm spray. No
more men for a while. She'd concentrate on her career.
She was twenty-six and she had plenty of time for them
later. No, not them, she corrected herself. She wanted
just one man: the right man. And children, too, of course.
She'd teach them how to bake cookies and paint and
sculpt and sing and dance waltzes. They'd have a blissfully happy, creative, colorful family...

Later.

She turned off the water, dried herself and went back
to her bedroom.

She slipped into a long, slim skirt with an exotic, mul-
ticolored design and topped it with a white silk T-shirt.
Humming a little tune, she brushed her hair until she'd
tamed it into some sort of order and tied it back with a
scarf the color of sandalwood. When at work she needed

to keep her hair out of her face, constrained in a scrunchy or a scarf, or it would end up in a bright halo of out-of-control curls, which made her look even younger than she already did. Blond hair and big blue eyes were the stuff of baby dolls. She made a face in the mirror, then put on some makeup and a pair of long, artsy earrings to add a touch of sophistication.

In the kitchen area she made coffee and contemplated the view from the window—an untidy design of brick walls and rooftops adorned with antennae, water tanks and chimneys. Here and there hopeful souls had created what looked like small gardens of potted plants.

Maybe she needed a change of scenery, to do something different, go somewhere else, get away from the men in her life.

Now where had that thought come from? Why would she even think about a change? She was happy. She loved her work and her roomy loft, she loved New York, and her friends. What else could a person want?

A sexy lover.

"No, I don't," she said out loud, glancing up at the sound of a door opening. Jason emerged from his room, dressed in gray sweatpants and a blindingly white undershirt. He was tall, blond and handsome like a Viking, but he had no social life to speak of. Why he hid his drop-dead gorgeous self from the world was anybody's guess.

"Good morning," Kim said cheerily, pouring him a cup of coffee. He looked bleary-eyed from lack of sleep and in need of some serious fortification.

"Thanks," he muttered, taking the coffee from her and leaning his hip against the counter to drink it.

"Sit," she suggested.

He raked his free hand through his thick hair. "I've been sitting all night."

While she'd been dreaming of her secret lover making

passionate love to her in a moonlit room, he'd been con-
quering the universe of numbers, or whatever genius
thing it was he did.

"When you dream," she asked on impulse, "do you
ever have the sense that there's a message in it?"

"I don't dream," he said.

"Everybody dreams," she returned. "You just don't
remember them necessarily."

"Which relieves me of the worry of interpreting
them." There was a flicker of humor in his deep blue
eyes.

Kim sighed. "I keep dreaming the same thing over
and over again and it's beginning to be a bit...con-
cerning."

"What type of dream?" he asked. "Is someone chas-
ing you? Are you falling down a bottomless hole?"

"No. It's more of a...romantic variety. A man I don't
know comes into my bedroom while I'm in bed. He
takes off his clothes—"

"You don't need to go into detail," Jason said, taking
a gulp of coffee.

Kim laughed; she couldn't help it. She'd done it on
purpose, wondering at what point in the story he was
going to stop her. "Haven't you ever had a really wonderful romantic or erotic dream, one that—"

"I told you, I don't dream." His face was expres-
sionless. "I've got to go back to work."

She watched his broad, retreating back and grinned.

The dream would not leave her alone; images of lovemaking floated into her mind as she worked, discussing
the designs for a line of lamps she had created for a
small, exclusive interior decorating firm, which was going to have them manufactured in Honduras.

How many tall, broad-shouldered men were there in
Manhattan? Kim had never paid any attention or kept

count, but now she saw them everywhere—walking in the streets, sitting in restaurants, riding in elevators, smiling down at her from billboards. She imagined them slipping into her room at night, getting into bed with her, stroking her. She couldn't help herself; it was embarrassing; it was awful.

The dream followed her as she rode home in a taxi, and stayed with her as she worked at her computer all afternoon. She kept seeing the tall dark man, kept feeling his tender touch, tasting his kisses. And the magic word he'd whispered, sounds that had no meaning to her, floated on the edges of her consciousness—tantalizing, mysterious.

She was going nuts. When a friend called and suggested meeting for dinner, she was so relieved with the distraction that she found herself leaning weakly back in her chair, gulping for air.

"Girl," she muttered, "get a grip on yourself."

Coming home later that night, Kim found a message from her brother, Marcus, on the answering machine. He had something of interest to discuss with her, he informed her, and suggested she call him at his office the next morning. In the grip of curiosity, Kim reached for the phone, hesitated and glanced at the clock. No, it was too late to call him at home. His wife Amy, heavily pregnant with their third child, would be asleep already and might wake up. Loving kindness won out over selfish curiosity and Kim put the receiver down with a sigh. The suspense was killing her.

Interesting. What could he possibly mean?

She got ready for bed, stumbling clumsily over her shoes, wishing she knew what Marcus wanted to tell her. At least she didn't have a boring life. She had a weepy stalker who sent her poems, a secret lover who visited

her at night and now a brother with a surprise. She
smiled as she rolled into bed. Life was pretty good.

She adjusted the pillow under her head, closed her
eyes and felt herself sinking like a rock into sleep.

Again that night the man came softly into her room,
took his clothes off and slipped into bed with her. Again,
she could not see his face.

"Hi," she murmured, burrowing into his embrace.
"I'm glad you're back."

"Yes," he whispered, and kissed her deeply.

Outside the window, the palm fronds stirred in the sea
breeze.

"Bahibik," he whispered, a mere breath of sound
feathering against her cheek, bewitching her.

She could not see his face, his eyes. With her hands
she touched the familiar outline of his cheeks and chin
and nose, traced his mouth with her fingers.

"Who are you?" she asked.

She could feel him smile. "You know who I am,
Kimmy, you know."

Kim got Marcus on the phone at ten minutes before eight
the next morning. He was always early at his office.

"Kim, remember you're always saying you want to
go back to the Far East one day? To work, for artistic
inspiration?"

Kim sighed longingly. "Yes, of course." If only she
could figure out how to do it—find a job over there,
inherit some money, win the lottery. The family had
lived on the island of Java, Indonesia, for four years and
had returned to New York when Kim had been fifteen.
She had loved the Far East, loved the international
school she had attended and the lush, tropical beauty of
the island. She had vowed she would go back when she
grew up, to study maybe.

"I'm waiting to win the lottery," she said to Marcus.

"Well, maybe you won't need to. Sam's back in New York, getting organized for..."

Kim's heart turned over and she didn't hear Marcus's voice anymore.

"Sam?" she echoed. "You mean *Samiir?*"

CHAPTER TWO

EVEN after all those many years, just hearing his name was enough to set Kim's pulse racing. She amazed herself. How ridiculous could a person be? She swallowed hard. Sam, short for Samiir, the Arab sheikh of her fanciful girlish dreams. She hadn't seen him in close to eleven years, not since she was fifteen and had been hopelessly, embarrassingly in love with him. He'd been twenty-three. Oh, Lord, she'd made such a fool of herself then.

Sam was Marcus's college friend and Marcus had brought him home for weekends and holidays when they'd been in graduate school. She'd been in awe of his dark, handsome looks and his calm, self-possessed manner; mesmerized by his enigmatic dark eyes that held a wealth of intriguing secrets and deep passions. He was so...*mysterious*.

Sam was in reality no sheikh but a full-fledged, passport-carrying American citizen whose Jordanian father and Greek mother had emigrated to the United States when he was ten.

"You remember Samiir, don't you?" Marcus asked.

She sucked in a deep breath. "Yeah, vaguely," she said casually.

Marcus gave a hearty laugh. "Sure, sure."

He wasn't deceived, of course. Unfortunately Marcus had been keenly aware of her amorous adoration of his friend, but not, she sincerely hoped, of her secret fantasies about him.

A hopelessly romantic girl with a fertile imagination, Kim had often envisioned Sam in long flowing white robes and a cloth covering his head. She'd made up elaborate scenarios of being lost in the desert and being rescued by Sam on a camel, who then brought her back to his tent, full of beautiful rugs and copper pots and large platters of sugary sweets and fresh figs. He always, of course, fell passionately in love with her.

Sam, however, had assured her once, when she had asked, that he had never owned any white robes or worn a cloth on his head. He had smiled magnanimously. "I was *ten* when I left Jordan, Kim. I wore jeans and T-shirts." Then he'd laughed. "Don't look so disappointed, kiddo."

Kiddo. He'd called her *kiddo.* She'd been crushed. Well, what could she expect? She was fifteen and looked twelve. She was short and skinny and wore braces on her teeth, and she was his friend's little sister.

Kim relaxed her fingers around the receiver and tried to focus on the conversation at hand. What had Marcus been saying? She wished her silly heart would calm down.

"What did you say about Sam being in New York?"

She'd heard little about Sam in the past eleven years; Marcus had once told her that he roamed the globe working for his family's international electronics company.

"He's here just for a month or so. Rasheed's Electronics is setting up another manufacturing company on Java and he's going to live there for who knows how long. He wants someone to get him a house and furnish it and hire servants and that sort of thing."

"Doesn't he have a wife to do that?"

"No wife," said Marcus. "Too much trouble, I think. All the demands she'd make on his time…and then she'd want children, just imagine." Kim heard the humor in his voice. Marcus was quite happily married himself with four-year-old twin boys, terrors, and the new baby was due soon.

"Anyway," he continued, "he mentioned Java and I thought of you, how you've always wanted to go back. You could do the job easily and you'd be really good, too. I don't know how much time you'd have for your own artistic and professional pursuits, but you could negotiate an arrangement, I'm sure."

The Far East. The island of Java.

Sam.

Setting up house for Sam.

Was this a fortuitous opportunity or a temptation to withstand?

A fortuitous opportunity, surely. Kim preferred to look on the bright and positive side of things; it made life so much more exciting. And hadn't she wondered, a couple of days ago, if she should have a change of scenery? A foreshadowing thought, of course. She believed in omens, in dreams, in intuition.

"He's coming to my office later this afternoon," she heard Marcus say. "We have some business to discuss. Why don't you come by here, say…six? I'd make it dinner, except he has to be somewhere else, so that's out."

"Six," she repeated. "Okay, I'll be there."

"She's perfect," said Marcus, looking at Kim and then back at Sam, who stood casually by the large window of Marcus's plush office, suit jacket open, hands in his pockets, radiating masculine appeal. He was observing her closely, seriously doubting her perfection, she was sure.

He was even more handsome than she remembered; older, more mature, his face all hard angles, his body lean and muscled under the expensive suit. He'd briefly taken her hand and smiled politely when she'd come in.

"Well, hello, Kim," he'd said. "What a pleasant surprise to see you."

"It's nice to see you, too," she'd replied, her heart about to jump out of her chest. She was grateful he hadn't mentioned how she was all grown-up now and not the little girl he remembered.

"She's absolutely perfect," Marcus emphasized.

Kim felt like a piece of merchandise and suppressed a grin. She tried to look serious and dignified, which wasn't easy. Being serious and dignified did not come to her naturally. She wished she hadn't worn the purple dress she had on, even though it was one of her favorites; it was too frivolous and too short and now that she sat there in Marcus's sumptuous office, facing the sophisticated Sam she wondered what had possessed her to wear it.

"I am," she said, summoning confidence, looking right into Sam's eyes. "Absolutely perfect." Her heart was doing a little dance of excitement. She wanted the job. She wanted to go to the Far East again. She wanted…

"She speaks Indonesian," Marcus went on. "How perfect can you get?"

"That's certainly an important asset," Sam acknowledged calmly. He looked so cool and composed, everything she was not. She pushed a curl behind her ear, wishing she had twisted her hair up in some elegant style instead of having it hanging loose in all its wild and untamed glory.

"And she's very good with people," Marcus continued. "She can even *cook!* Imagine a nineties' woman who can actually cook real food."

"Impressive, indeed." Sam's mouth quirked up at the corners as he met Kim's eyes. "Do you do windows?"

"No, but I can type," she said with mock seriousness.

"She's being modest," Marcus commented. "She

knows computers, word processing, how to find her way in cyber space, all that stuff. Very useful in case of an emergency.''

Sam's left eyebrow arched up slightly. "Really?"

Kim nodded. "Really." He must be finding it hard to believe that the dizzy little blond thing he had known eleven years ago was capable of anything so complicated as operating a computer.

Marcus leaned back in his leather chair. He was enjoying himself. "And she knows how to entertain. She gives fabulous parties," he boasted. "People even pay her sometimes to throw parties for them."

"And I can fix things around the house," she supplied. "Leaky faucets, electrical plugs, that sort of thing. I'm a handy person."

"She's not afraid of snakes and cockroaches, either," Marcus added.

"I'm a true Renaissance woman." She smiled brightly into Sam's face.

Sam was smiling now, and Kim's heart turned a somersault, much to her annoyance. Why was she reacting this way? He wasn't her type. She liked the more casual, easygoing type of man, the kind of man who wore jeans and sweaters.

But here he was, in his impeccable suit, his dark eyes mesmerizing her, and she felt fifteen again. She was an idiot.

"I'm impressed," he said. His voice was deep and resonant, a wonderful voice, that would wrap itself around your heart and give you warm fuzzy feelings. Actually maybe even more than warm fuzzy feelings. Oh, shut up, she said silently to herself. He's not your type. He's too cool, too self-contained.

"And she comes cheap," her brother was saying, as if he were selling her off like a slave trader, he a graduate of Harvard Business School.

Kim glared at him. "I am *not* cheap," she countered. "I insist on being paid fairly for my services." She groaned inwardly as she heard her own words. She sounded like a call girl. This whole exchange was beginning to have farcical overtones, which was not a good omen. She needed to present herself as serious, efficient and competent if she wanted to have any chance with the imposing Sam, the successful international business executive.

The problem was that, although she was perfectly efficient and competent, she simply didn't look it. Curly blond hair, big baby blue eyes and dimples just didn't add up to a serious appearance. She had trouble sitting still and she laughed too much. And nature had given her full breasts that were hard to hide. The truth was that efficiency and competency weren't qualities that came to men's minds when they first met her. It was a cross to bear sometimes.

Sam glanced at his watch. "I'll have to think about this," he said noncommittally.

He was not a man of many words, obviously; he hadn't been eleven years ago. Whatever he was really thinking now, he wasn't telling. Kim was annoyed. She liked people who were easy to read, easy to know. People who were not afraid of saying what they meant or felt. Sam was not one of these people.

What had she expected? That he'd say, *Excellent! You're exactly the person I've been looking for! I'll have someone get your tickets tomorrow, and let's talk, you and I, over dinner tomorrow.*

No, he was still the same introverted, reticent person, with those same eyes that often seemed impenetrably black, but sometimes glowed with sparks of secret amusement. He did have a sense of humor; he was just so...*quiet* about it. Often his face gave nothing away.

You'd just have to guess what went on in his mind. She didn't like all that still, deep water stuff.

But when he smiled at her—not the most exuberant smile she'd ever seen, but a smile nonetheless—her heart flipped.

"I have to go now," he said. "It was a pleasure seeing you again after all these years, Kim." It sounded sincere enough.

Two days later Kim still hadn't heard from him. All she had thought of for the last forty-eight hours was Indonesia, the job, feeling suddenly hungry for adventure. Ah, to eat *nasi-goreng* again, to hear gamelan music, to see the emerald rice paddies!

And she'd thought about Sam.

This was a mistake, of course, she was well aware. In spite of her teenage crush, in spite of the fact that he was stunningly handsome, not to speak of successful and well-manicured, he was not her type. He was too serious, too formal. And it took him much too long to get back to her with an answer. She was beginning to feel nervous and irritable. How long did it take to make a simple decision?

She decided to call him, which was easier said than done, but eventually, after verbally wrestling herself past a series of receptionists, secretaries and assistants, she got the busy man on the phone.

Her heart was beating fast. "Good morning, Sam," she said, trying to sound businesslike. "I'm sorry to disturb you, but I was wondering if you'd had time to consider giving me the job. You're leaving soon and it would be good to get started on some preliminary work as soon as possible."

A silence ensued. A short but noticeable one.

"Good God," he said then, "you weren't *serious,* were you?"

Her heart began a nervous rhythm. "Oh, yes, very," she said in as solemn a tone as she could muster. He thought they'd been joking. Well, she could hardly blame him, considering the way the conversation had developed, and the fact that he'd probably never taken her seriously in the first place. To him she was just Marcus's silly little sister who'd had a crush on him. Oh, Lord, she hoped he didn't remember the stupid, naive things she had done to get his attention, all those years ago.

"You want to come all the way to Java to set up house for me? Buy pots and pans, arrange furniture?" he asked, as if he were talking about scrubbing public toilets and mucking out pigsties.

"Yes, I would love to." She bit her lip.

Another brief silence as he was digesting this. "I don't believe that that would be what they call 'a positive career move' for you."

"I'm known for my bad career moves," she said impulsively. "Just ask my poor suffering father."

"Ah," he said succinctly, meaningfully.

"But somehow they always work out very well for me," she explained. "When I make decisions I use my intuition, my creative instincts, rather than my rational mind."

"And that is supposed to reassure me?" he asked with dry humor.

She kicked herself mentally. "I suppose not. I imagine your life is ruled by logic, reason, common sense and intellect."

"Employing those tends to work to my advantage, yes."

Kim made a face at the receiver. He had to be the most boring person in the universe, no matter how handsome he was.

"Well, don't worry," she said reassuringly. "I know exactly what I want and—"

"This is craziness, Kim," he said, interrupting her. "I'm not going to facilitate one of your harebrained schemes. I'll hire someone locally."

Kim grew hot with sudden anger. He was talking to her as if she were a child, not a grown woman who could make good decisions for herself.

"Sam, I'm not fifteen anymore," she asserted tightly, trying to control her anger. "This is *not* a harebrained scheme. I know what I want, and I want to go to Java and—"

"Kim, I have no time for this nonsense. I have a meeting to go to."

"Sam! I—"

"I must go," he argued. "Please, do excuse me."

And the busy man hung up.

Kim was so angry, she could scream. Who did he think he was to hang up on her? To not take her seriously? How dare he!

And who did he think he was going to hire locally? she thought later that day. The frustrated wife of an American contractor or consultant maybe. Someone with time on her hands because she couldn't get a work permit and have a job of her own. Somebody with no taste and no sense of design, Kim thought, sulkily, who'd cover the walls and beds and furniture with purple cabbage roses and put gaudy plastic flower arrangements everywhere and choose frilly pink lampshades and ruffled pink pillowcases. It would serve him right.

She visualized Sam's dark, manly head lying on a frilly pink pillow. In spite of her anger, Kim laughed.

Somehow she had to get Sam's attention. Kim lay in bed, wide-awake, staring up into the dark rafters, plotting, just as she had done when she was fifteen.

Phoning wouldn't work; he'd just find an excuse to end the conversation. She had to do it face-to-face, with no other people around to distract him or to use as an excuse to get away from her.

She'd ask him out to dinner.

Brilliant!

Not too forward a gesture, really. After all, she was no stranger. He knew her family well, had enjoyed much hospitality in her parents' house. He would be too much of a gentleman to refuse her invitation, surely? And once she held him captive, eating dinner in a public place, he wouldn't have any choice but to listen to her. She would be very professional and businesslike and convince him he wanted her to do the job.

The next morning she once again managed to get Sam on the phone, telling the slew of secretaries that she was his sister, Yasmina, calling internationally from Jordan on urgent family business.

"Sam, all I want is a moment of your time," she said hastily as he answered the phone.

"Kim," he stated, unsurprised. "I thought you were my sister, Yasmina."

"You don't have a sister, Yasmina," she informed him.

"Yes, I know," he said dryly.

"But that army of people you've got protecting you from the vultures preying on your precious time, don't know that," she continued smugly.

"I must speak to them." His tone held humor, which was reassuring. She didn't want anyone fired.

She sucked in a deep breath, fortifying herself with oxygen. "Sam, I'm calling to invite you out to dinner." So there, she'd done it, brazen woman that she was. "Any night this week, whenever it's convenient for you."

There was only the slightest of pauses. "I'd be de-

lighted to have dinner with you,'' he said then, ''but on
one condition.''

Her heart sank. He was going to tell her not to discuss
the job. ''What condition?''

''That you'll allow *me* to take *you* to dinner.''

She laughed, relieved. ''Sam—''

''I know what you're going to say, but let's not have
a big argument over it, shall we?''

''Okay,'' she said obediently. It didn't matter to her
who took whom. What mattered was that they sat at the
same table and that she had his undivided attention.

''Excellent,'' he said. ''How about tonight?''

Tonight. He wasn't wasting any time. ''Tonight is
good,'' she said.

His sister, Yasmina, indeed. Sam grinned as he put down
the phone, still hearing the echo of Kim's bright, sing-
song voice. He'd known it was her, of course—Marcus's
gregarious sister with the wild blond curls, the
Renaissance woman who was comfortable in cyber
space, who was not afraid of snakes and who could cook
''real'' food. And, reckless and impulsive as ever, she
wanted to come to Java and set up house for him.

It wasn't going to happen.

He glanced down at the file on the desk in front of
him and couldn't for the world remember what he had
been doing before her call had come through.

Ever since he'd seen her in Marcus's office a few days
ago, she'd been on his mind, which he'd found distracting in the extreme. He was busy and it had interfered
with his concentration. When she'd called the first time,
asking about the job, he'd been short with her, mostly
because he'd been irritated with himself for his inability
to stop thinking about her.

And now she had called him again and he knew he
wasn't going to get her out of mind.

Marcus's lovable, feisty little sister, all grown-up.

It hadn't taken great powers of observation to see she hadn't changed much. Spontaneous, vivacious and as charming as ever.

And tonight he was having dinner with her. It would certainly be interesting.

Kim stood in front of her bedroom closet and scrutinized the kaleidoscopic contents in despair. Her clothes were all so hopelessly unsuitable, but she had no time to run out and buy something new.

She loved clothes, but not the formal variety, which were fortunately not required for her work as a freelance commercial designer. She preferred fun, casual clothes, bright colors, playful designs. But for dinner tonight she needed something seriously sophisticated. She groaned with frustration as she rummaged frantically through the hangers hoping to find something halfway acceptable.

And there it was, in the very back: a neat little black suit—sober, proper, bought for the funeral of Great-Uncle Amos last year. She lunged for it with a sigh of relief and put it on the bed. From the back of the closet she excavated a pair of black pumps. Her jewelry box yielded simple gold earrings and a matching chain necklace, a birthday present from her conservative father. She was set.

Now her hair. She'd wear it up, out of her face. She grinned at herself. Boy, was she going to impress Mr. Samiir Rasheed with her businesslike image!

He came for her in a long, sleek limousine.

She was waiting outside the door to her building. The ancient cage elevator was out of order and she wanted to spare him climbing the stairs to the top floor.

The uniformed driver held the door open for her with a flourish and she slipped in beside Sam, taking in the television, computer, phone, fax machine, refrigerator and bar. A company vehicle, designed so the busy executives could continue doing their business while being transported from airports to offices to hotel suites, or perhaps their girlfriends' apartments.

"Hi," she said, trying not to sound too bright and peppy. Wearing conservative tan slacks and a deep blue blazer, he managed to look stunning, setting all her nerve endings atingle. She imagined that Sam would look stunning no matter what he wore.

She was sitting close enough to see the fine lines next to his eyes, to notice that his square chin was freshly shaven. Close enough to see sparks of mirth in the depth of his dark eyes.

"I hardly recognized you," Sam said. "You, in black."

"Actually I hardly recognized myself." Kim smoothed her skirt over her thighs. "I only wore this suit once, to a funeral and—" She stopped herself, and heard him laugh.

"A funeral? I hope wearing it now is not an indication of how you feel about having dinner with me."

"Don't worry," she assured him. "I hardly ever feel funereal about anything. It's too depressing."

"And you're not a depressed sort of person," he commented. "At least you weren't as a girl."

"No." This was dangerous territory. She didn't want him to think of her as the silly girl she'd been, the naive girl madly in love with him. That girl would no doubt have worn red tonight. Kim had the perfect dress in her closet—a deep, rich passionate red to express her real feelings about having dinner with Samiir Rasheed, the man who gave her foolish little heart the flutters, the man who rescued her from a tragic death in her fantasies. Of course they'd never been out to dinner together then, not just the two of them. They'd hardly ever been alone together anyplace, except that one time, in the garden of her parents' house, at night.

Not a good train of thought. She pushed it aside and glanced out the window at the neon lights, the billboards, the buses and taxis and people rushing along, all of it like a silent movie behind the dark glass of the air-conditioned limousine. An oasis of calm in the turmoil of the city.

Only she didn't feel calm. She had never before been aware of the power of the past, the pull of memories. It made her angry with herself. She'd been a stupid teen-ager, for Pete's sake! What she had been feeling then had no relevance to the present; she was no longer the same person. She was a grown woman now and she was not romantically interested in this cool, enigmatic man in his expensive clothes—no matter how drop-dead attractive and sexy he appeared. At the time Sam had been exotic to her, a volcano of controlled passion, ready to erupt....

She was aware of the faint scent of his aftershave, aware of sitting very close to him. It would be so easy to touch him—his arm, his hand, his thigh. Oh, good Lord what was she thinking? He was just another rich, workaholic businessman, a man who only knew about making money and had no talent for warm, intimate relationships with friends and lovers. He was most likely just a boring human being, a man without a wife and without a social life. He probably played solitaire at night while watching the stock market news on CNN.

Sure, a little voice teased her.

Mercifully it was not a long drive to the restaurant, a very upmarket place she'd never had the good fortune to visit.

"This is great," she said, studying the wonderful modern decor, the interesting art on the walls. The aro-

mas wafting around were promising; the menu alone was
a piece of art.

A waiter in a black suit came to take their drink orders. He talked with a French accent, a real one even.

Kim requested Chardonnay, and caught the dark
gleam in Sam's eyes.

"Ah, yes," he said evenly, "it's legal for you to drink
now."

She knew instantly what he was referring to. She'd
been well underage when she'd known him, which
hadn't kept her from secretly partaking of a couple of
glasses of champagne at her father's fiftieth birthday
party. And Sam had been there. It took an effort to force
down the heat of embarrassment that threatened to flush
her face.

The champagne had made her brave and wanton.
She'd more or less lured Sam into the garden, behind
the big hemlock tree, and thrown herself at him, or tried
anyway. She wasn't very practiced at that sort of thing.
It was mortifying even to remember it.

However, she was no longer a silly teenager. She was
twenty-six, a mature adult, and she had to convince Sam
of that so he'd give her the job.

"That was eleven years ago," she said with a dismissive little shrug, fiddling with her napkin so she
didn't have to look at him.

"Indeed," he said smoothly, not pursuing the matter
like a true gentleman. "So tell me, what has happened
with you in these past eleven years, apart from the ob-
vious?"

"Oh, well, in a nutshell?" She laughed. "I argued
with my father a lot, went to art school anyway, argued
some more, went to graduate school, argued some more
and then got a terrific job with an advertising agency
until I got bored working on soap campaigns and decided to go freelance to have more artistic freedom."

She stopped to take a breath. ''My father keeps thinking that I'm never going to have a real career, but all in all I'm doing quite well, and I enjoy my work. I'm good at what I'm doing and I've gotten great contracts. I'm working with architects and artists and interior decorators and—'' She was off and rolling, telling him about her work, and every time she wanted to stop, for politeness' sake—after all he had to get bored just listening to her—he kept asking more questions.

''And now,'' he said finally, ''you're ready to give all this up to come to Java for a temporary job finding me a house, buying bath mats and hiring servants?''

''Oh, but it's so much more than just that.'' It could be, anyway. ''You make it sound so...prosaic.''

''Setting up house usually is.'' No inflection in his voice.

She took a sip of wine and put the glass down. ''You told Marcus you wanted a home. You said you wanted something more than just a place to live. That you're tired of sterile hotel rooms and impersonal furnished apartments.''

He scowled down at his glass. ''Yes. I've been living like a damned nomad for the last ten years.''

Not in a lean-to or a tent, she was sure. No doubt he'd resided quite comfortably in expensive surroundings. But not in places he'd considered home apparently. It was hard to imagine. Even the shabby little apartment she'd had before she'd been lucky enough to get the loft, had been home. She'd simply made it that way, even buying in the beginning secondhand furniture. It had taken time and effort, but it had still been home—her things, her colors, her decorations and her choice of art on the walls.

''How long will you be living in Indonesia?''

''Five years, probably. Perhaps longer. And this time I've decided to get myself a place I can call home, not to rent someone else's house with someone else's furniture."

Only he did not have the time to invest in doing what was necessary—find a house, furniture, servants—Marcus had told her. Setting up a new company, managing and staffing it was going to take all his energies.

What he really needed was a wife, but Kim decided not to point this out to him; it might not be news to him.

So here she was in a classy restaurant in her funeral dress, trying to convince Sam that, since he didn't have a wife, she was the next perfect person for the setting-up-house job. She stared at his tie, a very nice one, thinking she might as well go straight for it. Just as she was about to launch into her appeal, the waiter came to take their order.

They ordered a first course, something duck-liverish that was artfully arranged on a big white plate and garnished elegantly.

"Food as art, I love it," Kim said. "It's almost too beautiful to eat—but I will!" She put her fork in the culinary art piece carefully and took a delicate little bite. It was delicious.

"Okay," she said, having finished it a while later, "give me the job and I will find you a wonderful house with a great veranda and furnish it and decorate it to your taste and specifications. I will hire you the perfect servants. And if you wish, I will even put on a big dinner or cocktail party when it's all done so you can show off your new home to your business connections and friends. I will do a fabulous job for you. I am very good at this sort of thing."

He observed her with a kind of curious speculation. "And your instincts tell you that leaving behind what you've built up in New York and trotting off to do this job for me will somehow further your career?"

"I never trot," she said, "But to answer your question, yes, in a way it will."

"In a way?" One eyebrow cocked, suspicions raised.

She fiddled idly with the little hoop earring in her left ear. "I have ulterior motives," she said with a bit of drama.

"Ah," he said meaningfully. "Now we're getting somewhere."

So she told him how much she wanted to go back to the Far East, how she loved Java, how there was nothing on earth greener than rice paddies, nothing better than... She went on for far too long, and he was quiet, listening intently as she told him of the wonderful art, the batik of Solo, the carved wood of Jepara, the fascinating way-ang plays that went on all night, the delicious food. She explained how good for her creativity it would be to live there, how much inspiration she would get. And when she finally stopped, she could feel her face, flushed and warm, and knew she must look like an excited child. She tucked a loose curl behind her ear and glanced down at her food, as yet uneaten. She felt his dark gaze on her as if it were a touch.

"Fascinating," he said.

She glanced up and saw him smile.

"All right," he said, "you've got the job."

Kim locked the door behind her and made a triumphant little dance through the living room. She'd done it! She waltzed into the bedroom and began to undress. And tomorrow she would see Sam again. They'd made plans for her to meet him at his office at six, since she'd be right in the area, and together they'd go to her loft, so he could see what she had done with the decorating and to discuss things further.

She caught her smiling reflection in the mirror. And

she had suggested, since it was evening, that he might as well stay and she'd cook them some dinner.

Too excited to sleep, Kim prowled around the living room in her peacock colored kimono, replaying the evening with Sam in her head as if it were a movie, recounting the conversation, seeing Sam's handsome face in her mind's eye.

"Why did you never settle down?" she'd asked. He didn't even own an apartment in New York, but lived in the company penthouse when in town.

"There was never much point," he'd said with a faint shrug of his shoulders. "I was free to do the work overseas, and most of the time I enjoyed the experience. There was never a reason to stop."

He had no brothers and sisters, she knew, and when his parents died when he was twenty, he'd lost his parental home. Kim remembered her mother being impressed by Sam's courteous appreciation of their welcoming him into their home during weekends and holidays, how he'd always brought a thoughtful little gift for her mother to thank her for her hospitality. Kim hadn't realized it then, but now, as she paced restlessly around the loft, she wondered if Sam had been lonely. Lonely for family and companionship.

And she wondered if he was lonely now, living like a global nomad.

Except for the widowed uncle who ran the company in New York, and one married Greek cousin, all his extended family lived in Jordan and Greece. Although he'd been thoroughly Americanized during his high school and college years, in his younger years he had lived and been educated in Jordan, but spending much time in Greece as well with his mother's family.

"I don't have a very strong sense of really belonging anyplace," he'd said over dinner, and his dark eyes had suddenly been full of shadows. She'd wondered what had been hidden in those shadows. Loneliness? It was an odd thought to have about Sam, who had always seemed so self-reliant, so...together. Yet who could tell what dwelled in the deepest part of people's souls?

Kim gave a little shiver. How awful it must be to not feel you belonged somewhere, to feel so rootless, to not even have a place to really call your own.

And now he wanted a house that was his, with everything in it belonging to him. A home.

And she was going to help him get it.

They met the next evening at Sam's office to discuss the job in more detail, then headed home to Kim's loft so she could show him what she'd done with her own place.

A clown in full circus costume was sitting on the doorstep when Kim and Sam arrived at her building. A sad clown, mouth curved downward, big fat tears painted on his face. He held a bouquet of huge rainbow-colored balloons. Several children had congregated and were laughing and teasing him.

It didn't take long to figure out what he was doing there and it wasn't a gig at a children's birthday party. I Adore You, Kim! one of the balloons read. Please Be Mine, was on another.

"Kim!" he called out as she emerged from the limousine. "Oh, please, Kim, listen to me, my heart is breaking!"

Hers was sinking, like a ton of cement. She was aware of Sam next to her, tall, silent, observing the spectacle. She didn't need this. A clown was not part of the plan.

"Tony," she said coldly. "This is enough, d'you hear? It's not funny anymore. Will you please just stop it?"

He began to sob, big, noisy, wet clown sobs. The children cheered.

"She doesn't love me!" he wailed between convulsions of grief. "I'm going to die of a broken heart!" The children laughed harder.

Kim took her key and pushed it into the lock, saying no more. She felt Sam behind her, knew he was wondering who Tony was. "Don't pay any attention to him," she said casually, loud enough for Tony to hear. "He's my stalker."

"Your *stalker?*"

They got into the elevator. "It's the newest craze, haven't you heard?" she asked breezily.

Sam frowned. "Who is this guy? What does he want?"

"I met him at a party three weeks ago, and he sort of trapped me in the corner of a room and bored me with endless self-involved stories about how he is misunderstood as an artist and an actor and how the world owes him respect and admiration. I found it a little hard to take, but I was trying to be nice and I tried to listen, and I think he thought I was...eh—"

"Charming?"

She made a face. "Something like that. I didn't want to charm him at all. What I really wanted to do was to get away from him."

"You're not having a lot of success," Sam said dryly. "So what else does he do besides play the clown?"

She shrugged carelessly. "Oh, harmless stuff. He sends me things—flowers, paintings, poems, love boat tickets. He leaves sappy messages on my answering machine, nothing dangerous. He's basically a frustrated, out-of-work, aspiring actor in need of a cause."

"And he sends you cruise tickets?"

"He has a rich daddy."

The clanging elevator struggled its way to the top floor. She wondered what Sam was thinking of the rat-

tling old contraption, what he would think of her rather
unusual living quarters.

She'd spent the morning housecleaning, shopping for
food and getting ready for Sam's visit. Her plan was to
cook something simple yet delicious, not wanting to
overdo things by offering him something extravagantly
expensive and ostentatious. Simple, yet elegant was the
key. She'd made a cold sauce of olive oil, Gorgonzola,
prosciutto, sun-dried tomatoes and garlic, to be tossed
with hot pasta and lots of parsley and chopped walnuts.
It was ready apart from cooking the fettuccini and as-
sembling the salad. The washed greens were in the
crisper, the lemon-ginger dressing was made.

She opened the door to the loft, looking forward to a
nice evening, and stopped dead in her tracks. A man lay
sprawled on her sofa, asleep—or dead, or in a coma, you
couldn't tell by the way he lay there—lifeless, motionless, his mouth slack, one arm dangling off the side.

CHAPTER THREE

IN STUNNED silence, Kim took in the man's appearance, all thoughts of a nice dinner with Sam fading into the distance. He looked like something that had crawled out of a swamp with his long, unkempt hair, his wild, woolly black beard, his old, ragged jeans. His shoes were off, muddy hiking boots the size of ocean liners. A bulky backpack, worn and faded, lay on the floor with half of its filthy contents spilling out onto her lovely Navajo rug.

She did not know this man.

Sam stood beside her in the door, calmly surveying the scene. For some reason she couldn't make herself speak. This was the moment for comic relief, to say something witty, something clever, something... anything.

"And who is this one?" asked Sam casually, as if he were already resigned to the fact that her life was littered with weird men, and that here was yet another specimen.

She swallowed hard. "I don't know," she answered, tonelessly.

A short, significant silence. "You don't know?" he inquired, as if he found it hard to believe.

"No." She didn't dare meet his eyes. She kept staring at the huge man on her sofa. His chest was moving up and down, so he wasn't dead. She supposed she should be grateful for small mercies.

So, what do I do now? she asked herself. What do you normally do when you come home and find a derelict passed out on your sofa? Call the police?

"How did he get in?" Sam asked practically.

She ventured a look at him. He looked very clean, very respectable, very…sexually appealing. Everything the comatose stranger was not. "I don't know," she said again.

"I think there's someone else here, too." Sam gestured casually toward the bathroom, where she now heard the noise of running water. A moment later the door opened and Jason emerged, naked apart from a blue towel wrapped around his hips. Water drops glistened on his manly shoulders. Apparently he'd just had one of his many showers to set him up for a night of serious brain work.

Jason was the only person she couldn't blame for making an appearance while Sam was around—after all, he lived here. However, did he have to show up in all his half-naked glory?

Her hopes of making a dignified impression on Sam had been duly crushed. Why had she even thought she could pull it off, she who had such undignified friends, led such an undignified life? How could she possibly expect him to take her seriously now? She'd asked him to her apartment for a civilized visit and instead he'd found an idiot clown on her doorstep, a swamp creature passed out on her sofa and a naked Adonis in her bathroom. All she really wanted was the chance to go back to the Far East for a while. Was that too much to ask? Why were the gods playing games with her, first dangling the opportunity in front of her, then yanking it out of reach? It just wasn't fair.

She didn't normally indulge in self-pity, but now she was truly being tested. She had the momentary impulse to just crumple to the floor, curl up in a ball and cry her heart out like a little girl. But that would not improve matters. Nothing could.

And she was right. The situation did not improve; it got worse.

"I hope it was okay for me to let him in," said Jason, indicating the inert body on the sofa. "He said he was your cousin."

"My cousin?" She only had two male cousins. One was a balding accountant in New Jersey, the other a red-haired student in dental school. "This is not my cousin. I don't know who he is." There was a desperate little shrill in her voice that embarrassed her.

The stranger stirred and opened his eyes. He gazed around dazedly.

Kim took a step forward on wooden legs, fury rushing through her, hot and fast. She glared down at him. "Who are you?" she demanded sharply. "What are you doing in my apartment?"

He focused his eyes and a slow smile crept over his hairy face. "You know who I am, Kimmy, you know."

She froze. There was something nightmarishly familiar about those words. And then it came to her.

The dream.

Her secret lover.

The stranger on the sofa reached out to her with his big hand, and she stepped back instinctively, nearly tripping over his boots. Boots like boats.

And then she knew.

Oh, God, she thought, it's Jack! Jack with the big feet. A horrifying thought occurred to her. Had she been dreaming of Jack? Of this repulsive man on her sofa? Of course he hadn't always been repulsive. He'd been clean and shaven once—seven, eight years ago when she'd been barely out of high school and hopelessly naive. She'd loved him for his charm and generosity, hoping marriage would change his excessive drinking and irresponsible behavior.

She closed her eyes. *I can't bear this,* she thought. *I want him out of here. Now.*

He kept smiling his dim-witted smile at her. It was

like some awful slow-motion film sequence. She saw Jason standing by the bathroom door in his towel, Sam in front of the bookcase, hands in his pockets of his trousers, silently observing the sorry scene, not interfering. And then the door flung open and the clown barreled in.

"Kim! I—" He glanced around the room, at the other men, then back at her, apparently stumped for words. Now all four were staring at her.

Jack shifted his big body on the sofa in an effort to sit up. He did not succeed and slumped back down. "Remember, Kim?" he muttered.

"No," she said hotly. *I'll kill him if he says anymore,* she thought wildly.

"We eloped, Kim. We eloped."

Her heart could not sink any lower—there was no lower place to go. But then, it didn't matter anymore. She'd had enough.

Kim gritted her teeth, took a deep breath and glared at Jack with all the ferocity she could muster.

"You're drunk," she said with disgust. "I want you out of here now, this minute!"

"Don't you remember, Kim?" he went on as if he hadn't heard her. "We eloped. Remember the island? It was so…the sea was so blue and the palm trees—" He stopped, as if talking was too much effort.

She didn't want to hear anymore. Not about the sea or the palm trees, not anything to do with her lovely dream.

"I want you out of here," she repeated. "Go home."

"Home?" His face was all dull confusion. "I want you back, Kim," he said plaintively. "I wanna be with you."

She decided not to react to this. "I'm going to call you a cab and you can go to your mother's house." She'd run into his mother quite by coincidence a couple of weeks ago, in Macy's, had chatted politely for a few minutes, gathering the news that Jack was on a trip around the world and was coming home soon. She'd never thought of it again. Thank you, thank you, she said to the gods, at least I know his mother is still around.

She made for the phone, only to find Sam was already doing the honors. He gazed at her as he was talking into the phone, ordering a taxi in a businesslike tone. His face was impassive, giving nothing away. She could only imagine what went on behind that inscrutable exterior, and it wasn't good, she was sure. She clenched her hands and turned away, gathering strength.

One down, one more to go. She turned to Tony, who had taken off his orange wig. "And you!" she exploded. "I've had enough of you! If you don't stop bothering me I'm calling the police, and I'll call my uncle, who's a pit bull lawyer, and you'll wish you'd never met me! Go get yourself a job! Get yourself a life! Out!" She marched right up to him, as if to push him out through the open door. He didn't budge, but gazed sadly down at her with his painted clown face.

"But you're my life, Kim," he pleaded.

"Get yourself a psychiatrist!"

He sighed. "I think I'll go to Hollywood."

"Now there's a good idea!" She pointed past him out the door. "It's that way."

He turned and shuffled out and she slammed the door behind him. She drew in a deep breath. She felt energized. Ah, a little fury did a person good!

Jack had hauled himself up in a semierect position and buried his head in his hands.

"Put on your boots," she ordered, pushing the offensive things closer to him with her foot.

He mumbled something inaudible and reached over to retrieve them. Jason came out of his room, dressed in jeans and a white T-shirt. She hadn't realized he'd left the scene. He moved past her toward Jack.

"Let me get his gear." Jason bent down, stuffed Jack's filthy belongings back into the backpack and hauled it out the door.

She glanced around for Sam. He had opened the beeping microwave oven and had extracted a mug, which he was delivering to the mumbling Jack. Warmed-up leftover coffee, Kim guessed.

"Drink this and make it fast." Sam's tone was impressive, full of cold authority.

Jack took the cup and drank it obediently while Sam towered over him.

Ten minutes later peace of a sort had returned to the loft. Sam and Jason had dragged the stumbling Jack and his gear into the elevator and into a taxi. Back in the loft, Jason had retreated to his room and Sam was sitting in a chair, observing her calmly. She was overwhelmed with a mixture of embarrassment and despair, but fought not to show it.

"How about a drink?" she asked, seeking refuge in social graces, wishing he would just magically disappear from her loft.

"Thank you, yes." Was there humor in his eyes? Surely she was mistaken.

"I have Chardonnay," she offered. She'd bought it to have with dinner. She didn't have anything else; she never drank the strong stuff.

"That will be fine."

Happy to have something to do she rushed into the kitchen, got the bottle out of the refrigerator and managed to open it without breaking off the cork or crashing the whole thing to the floor.

She took out a wineglass and filled it. Knowing she was in a gulping state of mind, she poured herself a glass of mineral water. She took a deep breath, straightened her shoulders and tried to look calm and in control as she handed Sam his glass.

"I'm sorry for the distraction," she said lightly, as if she had merely dispensed with a minor annoyance.

He gave a crooked little smile. "There was always a lot of distraction when you were around. I seem to remember you were often surrounded by a retinue of odd-ball friends."

"These guys are *not* my friends!" she said defensively.

"What about that Viking in there?" Sam gestured in the direction of Jason's room. "He seems decent enough."

"Oh, I never introduced you, did I?"

"It was a bit confusing, with your husband drunk on the sofa and him wearing a towel," he said forgivingly.

Under other circumstances she might have laughed, but not now. She glared at him. She was trying to rescue the embarrassing situation, but he wasn't going to let her. "Jack is not my husband and never was," she stated, feeling defeated already. And we were never together on any tropical island, either, she wanted to add, but didn't. They'd only looked at travel brochures and fantasized a lot.

Sam stretched out his long legs and made himself more comfortable in his chair. "He seemed to think you two had eloped."

"We did." Oh, God she didn't even want to think about her stupidity. She gulped down some water.

"You did?"

"We started out eloping, we just didn't finish."

"Ah," he said meaningfully. "What happened?"

She'd seen the error of her ways in the nick of time. Jack's car had expired from old age in the middle of a small town in New Jersey. Stranded by the road without money, listening to Jack suggesting they steal the car parked nearby, she'd finally seen the light.

Kim decided to give Sam the short version.

"His car broke down, and I got a headache."

He nodded understandingly. "That'll do it."

He was laughing at her. She'd had enough. Enough of him, enough of men in general. She came to her feet.

"You might as well go, too, Sam. There is no point in wasting your time here."

"You promised me dinner."

"I'll give you money for a hamburger." Her knees were trembling. She wanted him out. She wanted to be alone to lick her wounds in a dark corner.

One dark eyebrow lifted fractionally. "Why are you angry with *me?*"

"You're laughing at me! I hate men," she added to her own surprise. She had never said that before; it was a rather sweeping statement. "I'm going to ensconce myself in an ashram somewhere and learn to meditate and get in touch with my higher self and forget about men. No more men."

"I thought you were coming to Java with me." He took a leisurely drink of wine. He seemed so calm, so relaxed, she couldn't stand it.

"I imagine you're seriously regretting your decision, so I'll let you off the hook." She crossed her arms in front of her chest. She wished he'd get up and leave. She was feeling dangerously fragile, as if she might break down any minute. It was not a good feeling.

He rose and stood in front of her. "I thought you *wanted* to go to Java," he said quietly. "What's going on here, Kim?"

It was the tone of his voice, the quietness that suddenly made her throat close. Tears pressed behind her eyes. She could not believe it; she wasn't the weepy type. She hardly ever cried.

And she wasn't going to do it now, not even standing in the rubble of her hopes. She swallowed the constriction in her throat, blinked her eyes, composed herself. Well, she tried.

"You don't want somebody like me working for you. Somebody flighty and incompetent who holds company with clowns and derelicts." To her horror, her voice shook. Then, to her surprise, she heard him laugh.

"Ah, the drama, Kim," he said. "You didn't come across as flighty and incompetent at all when you booted those two jokers out the door. That was quite an impressive performance."

Well, it had been, actually, come to think of it. Her spirits lifted marginally.

Sam took her hand and smiled. "Fix me that dinner you promised me," he said. "And afterward I'd like to talk about my house."

For a moment her breath would not come. All she was aware of was his face and the warmth of his big hand holding hers, and his dark eyes as they gazed into hers.

I'm a fool, she thought. *I'm such a fool.*

"So, who shall we say I am?" she asked. "Your personal assistant? Your interior decorator? Your housekeeper?"

They were sitting on the sofa, drinking coffee. Kim was feeling better, much better. She'd cooked him her delicious little dinner, executed to perfection. He'd studied her portfolio, admired the decor of the loft and they'd discussed his requirements, likes and dislikes concerning dwelling places and their interiors. Her confidence had returned and she was beginning to feel like her normal happy self again.

"Somehow I don't think anyone will believe that," he said, giving her an amused look.

She could well imagine what people might think. Personal assistants, interior decorators and housekeepers were readily available locally and importing one from the other side of the world might raise questions. She smiled. "Saying I'm your sister, Yasmina, is not going to work, either."

He laughed, reaching out to touch her hair. "Not with your coloring, no."

He only barely touched her head and she hardly felt his hand, yet it seemed such an intimate gesture that her heart turned over in her chest and her breath caught in her throat. She looked into his eyes and couldn't tear her gaze away. She couldn't believe what was happening to her, she who had sworn off men.

"I suppose we could say you're my mistress," he said evenly, "which is not the truth, but they'd believe it."

The devilish glint in his eyes belied his level tone and she knew he was playing a game with her.

"*Mistress?* Me? Not on your life. I'm not going to be a kept woman, not even a pretend one."

He raised a brow in question. "Why not?"

"I find it distasteful," she said loftily. "In the extreme."

"Because it would imply you'd be having a sexual relationship with me?" He leaned back against the sofa cushions, apparently curious rather than offended.

Just like a man not to understand this. She sighed. "No."

"Oh, good," he said, quasirelieved. "I was beginning to think you found me unappetizing."

Oh, sure, she thought, looking at his handsome face, seeing the faint smile.

"Why then?" he asked.

"Because," she said patiently, "it would imply that I was getting paid or maintained in return for sexual favors."

"Ah," he said. "I understand. You have a high moral code."

A high moral code. It sounded so saintly. She didn't feel saintly in the least, but if he wanted to think that, okay, why not. She smiled breezily. "My mother taught me well," she said for good measure.

He laughed. "Of course, I should have known."

"However," she went on, "since I'll be looking for a house and furnishing it and doing all those cozy house-wifely things, we could just tell them I'm your wife. It will simplify matters." She could play the game, too. She smiled innocently.

His eyebrows shot up and she laughed. "Oh, don't you worry," she said sunnily, "I have no designs on you." She waved her hand in dismissal. "That was eleven years ago. Boy did I have designs on you then."

He nodded in agreement. "You owe me big," he said with dry humor in his voice.

The answer was not what she had expected. "Owe you?"

"You tempted me mercilessly and I had to be good."

"You had to be good?"

"You were my friend's little sister and I was offered hospitality in your home, which was very valuable to me, since your mother was an excellent cook. Needless to say fooling around with you was not a good idea. Apart from the fact, of course, that you were a mere child."

"And flighty and silly. Don't remind me."

"Okay," he agreed magnanimously.

"Besides, that's all in the past. It won't happen again."

"Good," he said deadpan. "It would be very disappointing to discover you hadn't fine-tuned your seduction techniques in the past eleven years."

There had to be something clever to say to that, but

her scrambling mind could not come up with it. Instead she shrugged lightly.

"Don't you worry about a thing. You and I..." She shook her head. "We're a bad combination, you know. We'd drive each other crazy."

His dark gaze held hers. "Most likely, yes," he said, and then he leaned closer and kissed her.

Lightly, softly. A kiss designed to tantalize and tease. Her heart rushed madly, and she was incapable of protest. She sat there, transfixed, overwhelmed by the sensuality of what he was doing, so simply, so easily.

Then just as swiftly as he had started, he stopped. Drawing back from her again, he smiled wickedly.

"Why did you do that?" she asked breathlessly, trying to add a note of outrage to her voice.

He grinned. "For all the times you wanted me to, and all those times I wasn't allowed."

Well, what could she say? Not much, being so out of breath. Not much, given so little time, because a moment later he did it again, as if he had every right, as if...

His mouth on hers, his arms around her, oh... She practically melted into him, she couldn't help herself. This is crazy, she thought, on the verge of not finding it crazy at all. I cannot let this happen. He can't just kiss me like that. Then again he could and he was doing it and she was letting him, her mouth softening, opening to him. Heat suffused her, dangerous, delicious. She didn't want to think anymore. She simply wanted to savor it.

"We could try it out for a while and see," he whispered against her lips.

Try out what? she thought dizzily.

She swallowed hard. "Try out what?" She asked. She could barely think. Oh, Lord what was happening to her?

His eyes gleamed. "Being married. Seeing how crazy we'd drive each other."

She stared at him, not sure her mind was working yet. "Married?" she asked stupidly.

"It was your suggestion," he said calmly. "We go to Java and pretend to be married, to make things simple."

"Oh," she said, aware that she wasn't sounding too bright. She eased away from him, struggling to gather her wits and think straight. She repeated in her mind what he had said: *Go to Java and pretend to be married, to make things simple.*

Her mind was beginning to clear. She moved away from him a little more, needing space, and manufactured a calm expression. Why not play along for a bit? It might be fun.

"It might cramp your style," she said levelly. "As a wife I won't tolerate your gallivanting around with other women. You know, the neighbors would talk."

His mouth twitched. "I don't gallivant. And what about you? Would it cramp your style?"

She waved her hand. "I'm off men," she said airily. "I've promised myself a man rest." Come to think of it, a pretend marriage might keep the men away from her—crazy stalkers and old boyfriends and new admirers. The peace would be blissful.

Maybe it was her lust for adventure. Maybe it was her intuition whispering encouragement. Maybe it was temporary insanity. Who cared what the reason—it suddenly seemed like a brilliant idea all around.

"Okay," she said. "I'll be your wife."

CHAPTER FOUR

KIM was savoring her first cup of coffee of the day as she gazed out over the wet rooftops of New York. Not an uplifting sight. It had been more than a week since she had found herself married, so to speak, and it had rained every single day, a drizzly rain designed to leach the good spirits out of a person. Kim's victorious mood, however, was not to be squelched. She was going to the Far East and she was exhilarated, rain or no rain.

It would have been nice, though, she had to secretly admit to herself, to have heard from Sam in the past week, which she had not.

He was very busy, she knew, getting organized for his new project. She herself had been busy as well, finishing her contracts and assignments and figuring out what to pack, what to ship and what to leave. Finding someone to sublet her loft had not been a problem. Fortuitously, if not tragically, one of her friends had materialized at her door in the middle of the night, wearing a raincoat over her nightgown, sobbing that she was leaving her man absolutely positively for good this time. Could she please avail herself of Kim's couch until she had found herself another apartment?

Kim told her she already had.

The phone rang and Kim put her empty coffee cup on the counter and picked up the receiver. "Hello," she said, stifling a yawn.

"Kim? Good morning," came Sam's voice. "Hope I didn't wake you."

Her heart did a little flip. "Not at all," she said, "*Selamat pagi* to you."

"Ah, Indonesian, I take it."

"I've been dragging it up and seeing what's left of it."

"I believe you mentioned you were fluent?"

"Close enough."

"I'm counting on it," he said dryly. "Now, your reservations have been made and your tickets should arrive in the next few days, along with a credit card in your name to be used for expenses and purchases related to the job." He sounded very businesslike as he continued giving her further information and, for all intents and purposes, she might have been talking to an assistant rather than the man himself. However, she did have to give him credit for talking to her personally rather than having a secretary doing the job for him.

"Thank you," she said, being equally polite. After all, she was his employee, or rather his hired wife. She tried not to think of the sensuous way he had kissed her.

"I'll be leaving in two days, sooner than expected," he went on, explaining that he had to go to Jordan to take care of family matters. "I'm afraid I won't have an opportunity to see you before I go," he said.

Some honeymoon this was, Kim thought and grinned into the receiver. "Not a problem," she said, trooper that she was. "I'll see you in a couple of weeks."

"I'm looking forward to it." His voice had lost its businesslike edge.

"So am I," she heard herself say.

It had been an endless journey, the last leg on a rickety plane that looked as if someone had built it from a hobby kit, and not too well. On the various planes she'd read, slept, played with somebody's cute, bald baby, watched a boring movie and chatted with her fellow passengers. Two of them, a Mexican and a Canadian, had given her their business cards with phone numbers, fax numbers and e-mail addresses all over the world and the invitation to call them anytime, anywhere, in case she changed her mind and wanted to have a meal, a night on the town, an affair, anything. She'd tossed the cards out at the first opportunity she had. No more men. No more relationships. No more agonizing over love and passion. She was free! Oh, bliss!

Having finally struggled out of the last plane into the hot sunshine of midday, she searched the arrivals lounge for Sam. Locating him was not a challenge. She saw him almost immediately and her heart lurched at the sight of the tall, broad-shouldered man in his impeccable tropical suit standing not far away, radiating confidence and sex appeal. His dark gaze caught hers and it seemed that for a moment everything grew quiet around her and it was just the two of them looking at each other while time stood still.

Then all was noise and tumult again. He was with her in a few long strides, kissing her briefly on the cheek. ''Hello, wife,'' he said in a low voice, smiling into her eyes.

The breath caught in her throat. She'd tried to put it out of her mind, hoping it might just quietly go away, this whole notion of her pretending to be his wife. She'd been crazy to agree to it. It was absurd, really, and she'd hoped Sam would be of the same opinion and would have conveniently forgotten about their ill-conceived idea. Apparently he had not.

The air was heavy and humid and she was sticky all over. Somehow she had forgotten about the oppressive tropical heat. She wiped her hair away from her damp face, watching Sam take charge of her luggage.

Moments later she was ushered into the comfortable back seat of a chauffeured car and Sam settled himself in next to her. It was blessedly cool and she relaxed against the backrest.

"So, how was your trip, or shouldn't I ask?" he inquired.

She made a face. "Don't ask. Every single plane I was on was as full as a cattle cart. It was claustrophobic." Then she grinned. "On the bright side, I got here."

"So you did. I was worrying you might have changed your mind."

She shook her head. "Not a chance." She glanced out the window, taking in the sights, familiar from long ago. Women in sarongs carrying baskets of produce on their heads. A food vendor with his rickety cart selling *sate,* small bamboo skewers of highly spiced meat. An old man with a yolk, brightly colored plastic buckets and dishpans and other plastic ware dangling from the ends.

"I'm so excited to be back," she said. "I can't wait to throw myself into things. The job I mean, finding a house, and everything."

Sam gave a half smile. "I do like your enthusiasm, but you're allowed a couple of days to recover from jet lag."

"I don't like doing nothing." She shifted restlessly in her seat, and he laughed, touching her hand briefly with his.

"Relax, Kim."

The hotel was not far away, a three-story building curved around a large central courtyard, which held a bar, an outside restaurant and a swimming pool, all deeply nestled in lush tropical foliage and flowers. It was a gorgeous place, the lobby full of exotic Indonesian art and she couldn't wait to have a good look at it all.

The hotel manager appeared in front of them, looking excruciatingly formal. He inclined his well-coiffed dark head. "Mrs. Rasheed, it is a great pleasure to have you with us," he said, extending his hand, and introducing himself to her.

Mrs. Rasheed. Well, there it was. She felt Sam's gaze

on her and refused to look at him. "*Terima kasi*, thank you," she said, smiling politely.

Her luggage was whisked away while they exchanged a few words with the man. Moments later they were meandering along the second floor gallery, past large, carved wooden doors and potted palms.

"I didn't get a key," she said.

"I have one for you."

She frowned at him. "You have my key in your room?"

He shook his head. "We're sharing."

She stood still as anger bubbled up. "Aren't we going a little far with this game?"

"You're my wife," he said matter-of-factly. "What would the neighbors say if we didn't live in the same—"

"That's ridiculous! I want my own room!"

He laughed and took her hand. "Take it easy, Kim. We're sharing a two-bedroom suite. No need to worry about your virtue."

He was making fun of her. Well, she was tired, hot, thirsty, and overreacting, not to speak of nervous, she, who was never nervous, being here with this big, tall, handsome man with his dark eyes that set her blood tingling; this man who was now holding her hand. She pulled herself free as they moved farther along the gallery.

"Here we are," said Sam, putting a key into a large, intricately carved double door. "Welcome to our temporary abode." The open doors revealed a huge sitting room with elegant Chinese furniture, flowers on the coffee table, soft carpeting underfoot and a magnificent view of the town and the China sea beyond.

"This is beautiful," she said, feeling her irritation dissolve. Her suitcases had already been delivered. Fast work for sure. A computer stood at the ready in a corner of the room, accompanied by a fax machine.

"It's all yours," said Sam, shrugging off his jacket and tossing it on a chair. He loosened his tie. "Feel free to use it for your own design work anytime you want. And it's hooked up to the internet, so you can e-mail your friends."

"Oh, Sam, thank you!" She was touched that it had occurred to him to get this set up for her.

"Wouldn't want you to feel out of touch," he said, opening a door. "And here's your room." It was off to one side of the sitting room and she walked in and glanced around. It was spacious and featured a huge, comfortable-looking bed. The color scheme was a cool white accented with bright touches of tropical green in the upholstered rattan furniture.

The room had its own adjoining bathroom decorated in a clean blue-green, the color of tropical seas. A basket of luxury toiletries perched on the wide marble vanity top. It was a lovely place and she couldn't wait to luxuriate in a long cool shower and get rid of the stale airplane smells that must be wafting from her every hair and pore.

Hands in his pockets, Sam leaned against the doorpost, observing her as she surveyed her new habitat. "Will this do until you've found us a house?" he inquired.

Found us a house.

She smiled sweetly. "I'll try to manage," she said, as if it would be a sacrifice to camp out in this place of comfort and luxury. "First thing I'd like to do is have a shower and lie down for a while."

Which she did.

It felt wonderful to get out of her clothes, to stand in the cool water and smell the fragrant soap. Wrapped in a big white terry bathrobe supplied by the hotel, she lay down on the bed, let out a deep, contented sigh and closed her eyes.

* * *

"Kim!" The voice came from far away. She felt someone touch her, a hand on her shoulder. Again the voice, calling her name.

She felt as if she were deep underwater, struggling to find the surface.

"Kim, wake up!"

She awoke with a deep sigh. She opened her eyes, and saw Sam's face close, bending over her.

She moaned and closed her eyes again. "I want to sleep," she muttered.

"You've been asleep for hours. You'd better get up now or you won't sleep tonight."

She didn't care. All she cared about was sleeping now. She felt his hand on her shoulder again.

"Have something to drink, Kim."

Drink. She was thirsty. She struggled into a sitting position. Groggily she ran her hands through her hair, which was a tangled mess, and as she did so she realized that the robe had fallen open and she was sitting there in front of Sam, her breasts exposed in their full nakedness, her hands up in her hair as if she'd intended to strike a suggestive pose. Sitting there like a Playboy bunny.

It was not one of her better moments.

From the beginning, all she had wanted was to make a dignified impression, to convince Sam she was a serious, competent person.

Obviously it wasn't happening.

Mortified, she yanked the robe closed. The belt had come undone while she was sleeping. She tied it again, pulling so hard she almost couldn't breathe. She wished she could come up with something witty to say to save the moment, something to assure him that this was not some cheap seduction technique, but her foggy mind was in no condition to produce something remotely funny or clever.

"Sorry," she muttered inadequately.

One corner of his mouth curved up. "Don't be," he said.

She glared at him, anger overpowering her embarrassment. "You probably think this is funny."

"Not funny, enjoyable."

She gave him a withering look and he laughed. "I am a man. Shoot me."

The last comment was so out of character, she almost laughed. Almost, but not quite. "Well, it's embarrassing," she said lamely.

"Don't worry about it. You're my wife, after all."

She rolled her eyes. "Oh, please."

This wouldn't have happened if she'd had her own separate hotel room, with her own door and her own key. He wouldn't be sitting here on the edge of her bed now, enjoying her unintended nudity and offering her advice. She felt again the apprehension about the whole marriage charade. What had possessed her to agree to it?

He handed her the glass. "Have some juice. Try to wake up. Twelve hours of time difference is a lot to adjust to."

She took a drink; delicious fresh fruit juice of some sort. She studied him over the rim of the glass. He had changed out of his lightweight suit, looking more casual now in khaki Dockers and a teal polo shirt. Like his hands, his arms were tan. Strong arms. A thin watch encircled his wrist. The top of his shirt lay open, revealing dark skin and a sprinkling of chest hair. It would be nice, she thought vaguely, to see more of his chest.

She was not pleased with this thought, but it had slipped out accidentally. She should be more careful. Sam's physical appeal was not a subject she wanted to dwell on.

He searched her face. "Do you feel well enough to

have dinner out, or would you prefer to order room service?''

Food. She wasn't sure if she wanted any food at all. She was only half-awake. And in this debilitating state of semiconsciousness she was forced to deal with a disturbingly sexy male sitting on the edge of her bed. She had no energy left to think about food. She wished he would leave her alone so she could relax and go back to sleep and not think about his naked chest.

She drew in a fortifying breath. ''I know you're trying to be considerate, but, really, you don't have to take care of me, you know.'' It was a feeble effort doomed to fail, but it was the best she could come up with in the handicapped state she was in.

He took the empty glass from her hand. ''Of course I have to take care of you. I mean, I *want* to take care of you. After all, you're my—''

''Don't say it,'' she said irritably.

''—my employee,'' he finished blandly, but she caught the spark of laughter in his eyes.

Taking care of employees did not normally involve sitting at their bedside offering drinks and inviting them out to dinner, but she decided not to point that out. She had no strength for verbal battle at the moment.

He stood up from the edge of the bed, towering over her. ''Well, I'll leave you alone.'' He glanced at his watch. ''I'm meeting someone for a drink downstairs in the courtyard. Feel free to join us if you like. Otherwise I'll be back later to see what you'd like to do for dinner. Would that suit you?''

She nodded gratefully. ''Yes, thank you.''

''If you want anything in the meantime, just call room service and have them put it on the account.''

''Thank you.''

He met her gaze and held it. ''Should I kiss you goodbye?'' he inquired politely.

"No," she said. "Not unless you want to drive me crazy."

A flash of white teeth. "Don't give me any ideas."

She glowered at him. "Refresh my memory, why are we doing this again?"

"To make things simple. It was your suggestion, I believe."

"It's nonsense, really. I can't imagine...well, never mind. You already started it so there's no turning back now." She had agreed to it, had thought it was a good idea even, to keep other men away from her. What a laugh that was.

"No turning back now," he agreed.

"We're going to drive each other nuts, you know," she said morosely.

"That was one reason," he said. "To try it out to see."

"It was a stupid idea."

"You're stuck with me now, sweetheart."

"Don't sweetheart me! I don't like it!"

He glanced down at her, his face even. "What would you prefer? Darling? Honey?"

"No!"

He laughed out loud.

"You think this is funny? I think this whole idea is mad. I must have been out of my mind to agree to it." She moaned and buried her face in her hands.

"You're just tired," he said soothingly. "Get dressed and come down for a drink. You'll like James. He'll perk you up."

She glanced up at him. "I'm in no mood to be perked up," she replied, testily.

He gave her a clinical look. "You're very cranky when you're out of sorts, aren't you? I don't know that side of you."

She gritted her teeth. "Get out of here, Sam!"

He inclined his head. "As you wish, darling. See you later."

He made for the door with a few long strides. She wanted to throw something at that strong, sexy back of his—a high-heeled shoe, a poisonous spear. She chuckled. Lucky for him, she didn't have either one handy.

CHAPTER FIVE

IT WAS not, Kim reflected with amusement, an auspicious beginning of a marriage to feel the desire to do your husband bodily harm. She leaned back against the pillows and closed her eyes. It wasn't like her to get agitated so easily. Well, she wasn't herself, really. She had traveled to the other side of the world, had skipped an entire night's sleep and her whole system was out of kilter. No wonder she was a bit testy.

She sat for a while, gathering the energy to get out of bed, which eventually she managed to do. Then, gaining momentum, she started unpacking her suitcases. She should get dressed, too, she supposed, and do something about her hair. She looked like a scarecrow.

So, what to wear? It was almost dark outside and it was barely six. She glanced out her window and saw the courtyard below and people sitting around casually, talking and laughing. Candles flickered on the tables and waiters with trays wandered around serving orders. She didn't see Sam. Observing the lively scene below, she felt the sudden urge to vacate the empty suite and find a little cheer for herself, not to speak of fresh air. She was beginning to feel somewhat restored.

She'd find Sam and this James guy and have a drink. A cool glass of mineral water to rehydrate herself. After all those hours in the air she was feeling like a dried prune in need of plumping.

She slipped into a cool, white dress, which made her look rather virginal and she grinned at herself as she piled her hair on top of her head. She put on white sandals that showed off her coral polished toenails, and after a few minutes of putting on her makeup with various pencils and brushes, she felt presentable again. Off she went, out of the heavy, carved doors, along the breezy gallery in search of a little entertainment.

She located Sam at a corner table, talking to a man with longish blond hair, who wore white shorts and a black T-shirt.

"There you are," said Sam, looking pleased. "Kim, this is James French. James, my wife, Kim."

My wife Kim. Oh, Lord this would take some getting used to. Kim extended her hand and smiled demurely. James got to his feet and, taking her hand in a firm grip, flashed her a gorgeous, toothpaste smile. "Surprise, surprise," he drawled. He had green eyes, she noticed, and they had a decidedly speculative look in them.

Sam pulled out a chair for her and a waiter came rushing over to take her order. "Mineral water, please," she said. "The bubbly variety, with a slice of lemon."

"So," said James, leaning back in his chair and regarding Sam with undisguised curiosity. "This is news, my friend. A couple of months ago you were firmly *un*-hitched."

Sam's mouth quirked at the corners. "Well, you never know," he said vaguely.

"It all happened rather suddenly," Kim said lightly, leaning back in her chair and crossing her legs at the ankles.

"You met in New York?" The green eyes observed her with interest.

"Yes, well, actually we knew each other years ago, but when we saw each other again..." She let her voice trail away, not sure how to finish the sentence. Where was all her imagination when she really needed it?

"Passion flared," James finished for her, grinning. "Sam, my friend, you are a lucky man."

"Yes, I am," said Sam. He smiled at Kim. "You seem to be feeling better," he observed.

She wondered how you were supposed to play the role of a loving wife. She offered him a repentant smile. "Yes, and I'm sorry I was such a grouch earlier on." She turned to James. "I just arrived this afternoon, you see. Jet lag makes me cranky and I wasn't very nice."

"Really?" he said blandly. "And that after you hadn't seen each other for a couple of weeks?"

Oh, she was blowing it already. Needless to say a new bride should have been wild with passion rather than cranky with jet lag. She was rescued by the appearance of the waiter bringing her water.

James was an international business consultant, she discovered in the course of the conversation. He didn't look like the type, but then, life was full of surprises. On several occasions he had done work for the Rasheed Company, as he was doing now.

She liked his easygoing manner and he seemed to like her, too, drawing her out with funny jokes and stories. Sipping her water, Kim found herself talking and laughing and forgetting for the moment that she was exhausted. When Sam excused himself to make a quick phone call, James leaned forward in his chair and looked right at her, a gleam in his eyes.

"So," he said, "what's the story?"

"The story?"

"You're not married," he stated.

She widened her eyes in mock surprise. "What makes you think that?"

"Oh, lots of intangibles." He grinned. "And one in particular." He picked up her left hand and stroked her empty ring finger. "No wedding ring."

Stupid her. She'd never given it a thought. "Oh," she said casually, slipping her hand out of his grip. "I forgot to put it back on. It's in my room. I'm not used to wear-ing it yet.''

He nodded. ''Sure,'' he said with feigned understand-ing.

She stared right into his green eyes, daring him to contradict her, and he laughed.

''I like you, Kim,'' he said.

''Thank you.'' She did not return the compliment. Oh, dear Lord, not again, she thought, thinking of the men in amorous pursuit of her on the plane.

James's eyes narrowed with speculation. She took a sip from her water. Here it comes, she thought. And I didn't do anything. I didn't lead him on. It's not my fault.

''Now, if I called you tomorrow,'' he said right on cue, ''would you have dinner with me?''

''No,'' she said, smiling sweetly, ''I wouldn't.''

He grinned. ''Sorry, just asking.''

Just asking my foot, she said silently.

Sam arrived back at the table and James came to his feet. ''I must be off.'' He extended his hand to Kim. ''It was a pleasure meeting you.'' There was a devilish gleam in his eyes. He gave Sam a semisalute. ''Good luck with married life. See you around.'' He turned and loped out of the courtyard.

Sam was still standing. ''Shall we?'' he suggested, reaching out a hand to her. Taking it, Kim got to her feet.

He did not let go of her hand and they crossed the courtyard and entered the lobby. She'd hoped to have a man-free period in her life and here she was, walking hand in hand with a pretend husband, having just been asked to dinner by another man with amorous intentions. It was too ridiculous for words and a chuckle escaped her. She slipped her hand out of Sam's grip, and he slanted her a curious look.

"What's so funny?"

"I was thinking that coming here would make it easier for me not to get involved with men, especially if I pretended to be married. Well, I didn't even make it into the country without two guys on the plane giving me their business cards and a variety of invitations, and now, well, I've been in the country for half a day and..." she sighed and laughed at the same time.

"And James made a pass at you," he finished for her, apparently not surprised. He opened the door to their suite and Kim waltzed in and tossed her bag onto the sofa.

"He doesn't believe we're married and he asked me to go out for dinner with him tomorrow night."

Sam didn't seem noticeably perturbed. "James never was fooled easily," he commented, closing the door behind him. He gave her a questioning look. "So, did you accept?"

"I'm not even answering that," she said, rolling her eyes. "I intend to be a very faithful wife, you'd better believe it."

"That's a relief. James is quite a charmer."

"Oh, I can handle his kind." She dropped down onto the sofa and slipped off her sandals. "I just can't believe it," she said, shaking her head. "Why did he do that? Why those two guys on the plane? I mean, I'm *not interested.* I'm not sending signals, at least not that I'm aware of. I'm supposed to be *married,* for heaven's sake. What am I doing wrong?"

He stood by the window, hands in his pockets, regarding her with amusement. "You're not doing anything wrong, Kim. You're just you."

"And what does that mean?"

"Men are attracted to you for who you are. You're vivacious, funny, easy to be with. You have a natural charm and a natural sexiness. You draw men to you, inadvertently.''

Was that what he was experiencing? Her mouth went suddenly dry. She had to say something, she realized after a moment.

''That's awful,'' she said, and then, hearing her own words, she laughed. ''Oh, God, what am I going to do?''

''Do about what?''

''About inadvertently attracting men. It's not what I want, it's not what I intended to happen with James.''

''I don't think that you can change your basic nature and personality.'' Humor colored his voice.

''I can try,'' she muttered, glancing down at her bare feet, wiggling her toes. ''I can talk less and be more reserved.''

He laughed. ''Not a chance.''

''I can crawl into a cave and never come out.''

''But you'd have such a boring life,'' he said, sitting down next to her. ''Or would you allow me to join you?''

She laughed helplessly. ''I'm hopeless. Poor you, you've got yourself a hussy for a wife.''

''I said nothing about your being a hussy. I said you have a natural charm and a natural sexiness.'' He leaned a little closer, capturing her gaze with his. ''You are a real woman, Kim.''

She scooted away from him into the corner of the sofa, half-scared, half-amused. Her heart was racing, yet she wanted to laugh about the absurdity of it all.

''Not you, too,'' she said, faking a note of despair in her voice.

''Of course me, too.'' He took her hand. ''You're my wife.'' His tone was light, yet for a fraction of a moment she caught a glimpse of something dark and smoldering in his eyes. Her heart made a nervous little leap.

''Don't play games with me.'' She slipped away from

him and got to her feet. "I'm hungry," she stated briskly. "Let's go out to eat."

He came to his feet as well, towering over her, all cool composure. "Excellent idea," he agreed.

The next afternoon an enormous, opulent flower arrangement was delivered to the suite. Kim gazed with awe at the exotic flowers as their perfumy scent filled the room.

She found the little card tucked in the foliage and opened it. They were from James. She scanned the message.

Dear Kim, please accept these as a gesture to convey my apologies for my inappropriate behavior yesterday. I'd be delighted if you and Sam would join me and some friends for dinner Saturday night. Please give me a call to confirm.

Kim wasn't fooled. The flowers were much too extravagant, the language too formal.

Sam came back to the suite an hour later, raising his eyebrows at the sight of the massive floral display on the coffee table.

"Well, what Don Juan did you charm today?" he asked casually.

She faked a sad face and sighed. "Nobody new today. I think I've lost my touch. These are from James."

"James? Well, well. Fancy that."

She handed him the little card. "He's apologizing for making a pass at me last night, only he doesn't use that term."

He read the note. "Would you like to go out to dinner with him and his friends?" he asked, referring to James's invitation.

"I'd like to meet more people," she said, which was the truth. She could handle James.

"Okay, I'll call him." He tossed the card on the coffee table. "And now I'll shower and change, and then we'll venture out to find some dinner."

Sam stood in the shower, realizing he was grinding his teeth and his body felt tense. Damn James and his flowers—he just couldn't resist making a move on Kim. It was all a sport to James, he was sure, but just the same, Sam felt like punching his lights out.

The uncharacteristic fierceness of his emotions caught him up short and for a moment he stood motionless in the streaming water, trying to calm himself.

He hadn't felt like this for…how long? Why was he getting agitated about James, of all people?

Was he *jealous?*

Kim looked up from her magazine when Sam came back into the room a while later. He crossed to the small bar, his body moving with an ease and confidence that was completely natural and disturbingly male. Kim felt the instant stirring of her senses and wished she didn't.

"Would you like something to drink?" he asked, taking a bottle of water from the small refrigerator.

"Water is fine." The heat made her thirsty. Kim watched him as he poured them both a large glassful, wishing she wasn't so aware of him as a man. Wearing white trousers and a royal blue, open-necked shirt, he looked cool and clean and much too sexy for her comfort. Why couldn't he just be ordinary looking? she thought. But there was nothing ordinary about Samiir Rasheed, not about his strong, square-jawed face nor about his lean, broad-shouldered body.

"Where would you like to go for dinner tonight?" he asked.

"Somewhere local and rustic." Yesterday they had eaten in a Western-style restaurant—wonderful food, soft music, elegant atmosphere. Very restorative for a

person suffering from jet lag. Now she was ready for the
local fare. Lots of red pepper and garlic and noisy music
to go with it.

Humor flickered in his eyes. "Local and rustic? You
mean a *warung massakan*, out in the open? Formica tables, rickety chairs, oil drum grills?"

She nodded eagerly. "Spicy grilled shrimp, *sate* with
peanut sauce, the works."

"You've got it."

He put both glasses on the coffee table and sat down
next to her on the sofa. "But first, I have something for
you," he said, reaching into his right pocket.

"Oh? Really? What?" He'd caught her by surprise.

"It's something I want you to have." He handed her
a small, beautiful silk jewelry box.

Holding her breath, she opened it up, finding inside,
nestled in rose-colored silk, a diamond ring. It was simple, elegant and very beautiful.

"Oh, my, that's gorgeous," she said, letting out the
breath she'd been holding.

"I'm glad you like it."

"Oh, I like it." She glanced up at him. "I only hope
it's a pretend diamond to go with the pretend marriage."

He gave her a crooked little smile. "No wife of mine,
pretend or otherwise, wears a fake diamond." He took
the ring from her. "Let's do this properly." He took her
left hand and slipped it onto her ring finger, where it
glittered brightly.

She stared at his big hand, holding hers, at the spar-
kling ring on her finger. She swallowed. "This wasn't
necessary, Sam. A plain gold band would have done, I
mean…"

"I wanted you to have this one." And then he pulled
her into his arms and kissed her. She gave a soft little
moan, wanting him to stop, not wanting him to stop. She

moved her mouth away from his with a strength she didn't know she had.

"Sam, please," she whispered.

"Sam, what?" he asked, his arms still around her.

"We can't do this," she said shakily. It was too dangerous a game.

"Why not?" His dark eyes looked right into hers, brooding, seductive. It was awful.

"I don't like playing games, Sam."

"Who says I'm playing games?" he asked softly. "I like kissing you."

"I'm here to do a job," she said desperately. "And I don't want to get involved again for a while. I'm always picking the wrong men and—"

"And you think I'm wrong?"

"We're wrong for each other," she said, proud of her diplomatic answer.

"We don't know that yet. You've only been here for a day and a half." There it was again, briefly, that hungry look in the depths of his eyes. Was she just imagining it?

She swallowed hard, trying to think of something to say that would refute his logic. Logic wasn't her strong point, which didn't help. She was in the grip of her emotions, her thoughts were in turmoil and she was fighting the beginnings of what might be a panic attack. Well, maybe not.

"Give us a chance, Kim," Sam said, then the phone rang, just as if in the movies, and her chance to really turn him down was lost.

Sam got up to answer the phone and Kim fled to her room, the ring glittering on her finger.

On Saturday night they met James and his friends at a restaurant in town, another opportunity for Kim to play her role as Mrs. Rasheed, complete with ring.

"Have some of the *rujak,* darling," Sam said to Kim, holding the bowl with the spicy fruit and vegetable salad in front of her. He smiled at her lovingly, while on her other side James put a hand protectively on hers.

"It might be a little spicy for you, Kim," he said with concern.

She pulled her hand free and shot him a murderous glare, not caring that the two other guests, his friends sitting straight across from them, were witness to it. For propriety's sake she had to put up with Sam's gallantries, but she didn't have to with James. He was seriously getting on her nerves.

No sooner had they settled themselves at the table in the restaurant an hour ago, James had showered her with attention, smiles and compliments. In response to James's loving kindness, Sam had started in on her as well, playing with her hand, putting an arm around her shoulders, whispering seductively in her ear. Unfortunately, this had a unsettling effect on her, and he knew it. She wished she could stay stone-cold under his touch, but her body had a mind of its own. Once in a while, for James's benefit, and to play her part, she'd smile nicely at Sam.

She'd barely taken a few bites of the *rujak* when James, leaning his face close to hers, took her left hand. "Lovely ring, Kim," he said.

She yanked her hand free and, facing him squarely, kicked his leg under the table. He grimaced painfully, which she found gratifying.

"Stop flirting with my wife, James," Sam admonished, cucumber cool. "Or I might have to fire you."

James gave a long-suffering sigh. "I can't seem to help myself. The devil makes me do it."

They were having a friendly competition, those two, to see who could be the most attentive, the most charming, the most seductive. It was truly exhausting.

None of this of course escaped the two sets of eyes across the table.

James's friends, Maya and Joel, were a young American couple who'd started a business some years ago exporting crafts and artwork to Europe and the States. Maya had offered to show Kim around the town, help her with her search for a house and give her assistance with whatever she might need.

Maya was tall and thin, had very short, black hair, and brown eyes that looked huge in her small face. She had a hungry look about her, like a beautiful Italian fashion model. However, she wasn't starving herself going by the impressive amount of food she was consuming tonight.

Kim tried to ignore the two men on either side of her and concentrated on making conversation with Maya, which was not easy with Sam playing with a strand of her hair and pretending to be the loving husband who couldn't keep his hands off his wife. Then again, maybe he wasn't pretending.

This thought did not help her already overtaxed sensual awareness of him in the least. Her head began to feel a bit dizzier, her heartbeat grew even more frenzied. When she couldn't stand it any longer, Kim excused herself and stood up from the table. Maya followed suit. Together they strolled to the ladies' room.

"Your husband is drop-dead gorgeous," said Maya, looking at Kim's reflection in the mirror.

"Yes." What else could she say?

"And James is quite a guy, too," Maya added.

"Quite a guy," Kim acknowledged dryly.

Maya's big brown eyes looked at her speculatively. "Would you like to switch chairs when we get back?"

Kim chuckled; she couldn't help it. "Aren't you enjoying the show?"

Maya laughed. "Actually I am, but I'm not sure you are."

Well, it was beginning to strain her reserves of patience and energy. She'd come to Java with the intention of being free of men and here she was fending off two at the same time.

Kim shrugged lightly. "James is playing a game with Sam." An idea occurred to her as she spoke. It was not a very dignified idea, but she might as well give up on the idea of trying to be a dignified person. It was a lost cause. She grinned at Maya. "I'm about done being his little toy. Thanks for the offer, but I'll sit in my own seat. He can play games, but so can I."

Back at the table, she smiled happily at no one in particular and sipped the coffee that had been poured for her in her absence.

Next time James made a move on her she was ready. She picked up a full glass of water and emptied it over his blond head.

Coming to her feet, she smiled down sweetly at the stunned and dripping James. "Thank you so much for inviting us, James. It was a lovely dinner." Tossing her hair back, she beamed up at Sam, who had also risen to his feet.

"Let's go home, darling," she said. "I'm exhausted."

Jet lag conquered and energy restored, Kim embraced her wifely duty of setting up house with enthusiasm, beginning with the search for suitable living space.

Sam had made a car and driver available to her and she and Maya cruised through the town, exploring the various neighborhoods, the open market, the shops. Kim was enjoying herself. She liked Maya, who had a funky sense of humor and had much admired Kim giving James a good dowsing, which, in her opinion, he had richly deserved. Maya was a treasure trove of knowledge concerning the town and the island and, more than anything, Kim was grateful to have some cheerful, non-stressful female companionship.

Most nights she and Sam had dinner together and she'd talk enthusiastically about the adventures of the day and he would listen, throwing in a few words here and there. Often she'd catch him silently observing her with a look in his eyes that was not at all businesslike. She tried to ignore it.

One day she was rather late coming back to the suite. Rushing along the gallery, she came flying into the room, finding Sam already there.

"Hi!" she said. "Sorry I'm late."

Sam was sitting in a chair reading some documents. Mozart was playing in the background. It was a very civilized, tranquil scene.

"Not a problem," he said graciously.

"I saw some great houses today!" She launched into a description of the various places, asking him what he thought of this and that. She rambled on about some interesting people she'd met, and asked if they could have dinner with them some time. Finally she stopped herself, realizing she'd been going on for quite some time. Sam was looking at her patiently, papers on his lap.

She sighed. "I knew this would happen, you know. I'm driving you crazy, aren't I? I destroy your lovely peace and quiet by demanding all this attention, wanting your opinion and asking you to make choices. I talk too much, I laugh too much. So I'll quit right here."

"Good," he said good-humoredly. "Then I'll be able to finish this."

She gathered her purse and shoes, which she'd kicked off and was about to go into her room to have a shower and change into clean clothes for dinner when Sam glanced up again from his reading.

"Am I driving *you* crazy?" he inquired, as if it had only just occurred to him that she'd indicated a mutual situation not so long ago.

She nodded. "Yes," she said simply. Oh, yes, yes.

He kept looking at her as if expecting her to say more. She was not prepared to elaborate without his requesting it.

"How?" he asked. He put the documents aside as if ready to give the discussion his full attention.

"You don't talk," she informed him, dropping shoes and handbag. "You don't express your feelings, you don't tell me what you think and feel." She frowned. "I sound like a complaining wife, don't I?"

He nodded sagely. "Right."

"Well, since I'm not really married to you it doesn't matter in the least. You don't have to tell me your innermost feelings." She plopped into a chair with a sigh. "But it's what I like, you know. I like people who are up-front, who tell me what they think and feel. Then I know and I don't have to guess."

"Like that clown on your door step: *'My heart is breaking! You are my life!'*"

"You're not being fair! He was a nutcase!"

He was not impressed by her objection. "What about that almost-husband of yours? He loves you, he wants you back. Was he an example of sanity?"

She glared at him. "I hadn't seen him in eight years or so. I didn't even recognize him. And anyway, he was a bad mistake. I told you, I'm not good at picking men."

"But they expose all their inner feelings to you, and you like that."

"Right. That's why I knew I had made a mistake with Jack, way back when." She gave him a challenging look, pleased with her own logic.

He laughed.

"Why are you always laughing at me?" she said, annoyed.

His eyebrows shot up. "I'm not laughing *at* you. It's not negative. I'm laughing because you amuse me."

She amused him. "Gee," she said, "so I am your entertainment. Should I be flattered?"

"I didn't say it to flatter you," he said levelly. "It's just how it is."

"Well, it's...vexing, your laughing when I'm not sure what you're really thinking."

"Vexing? An interesting word."

"I read it in an English novel last night. I thought I'd try it out. And don't laugh."

He laughed. "So my laughing vexes you."

"Yes. I always have this idea that you're thinking things about me that you're not telling me, like you're *observing* me, as if I'm some sort of secret scientific experiment."

"You're not a scientific experiment. You're a wifely experiment and I find it fascinating to live with you and watch you go about your activities and listen to you talk about the rigors of your day." His eyes gleamed with humor, and something else, something more elemental, something...predatory.

She jumped to her feet. She needed to leave, before she got drawn in by those eyes, the feelings he stirred in her, that treacherous need to find out what lurked in the depths of him.

But of course she already knew. There was passion there, and fire.

And it scared her to death.

Getting burned, after all, was not a pleasant experience.

"Leaving?" he asked innocently. "Did I vex you?"

Pretending not to hear, she sought refuge in her room.

* * *

"I've been thinking about what you said a few days ago," said Sam one evening.

"And what was that?" She'd said a lot of things, which was usually the case when you talked too much. She had trouble remembering what she'd said an hour ago, let alone several days ago. Every day she tried not to talk so much, and every time she forgot, gushing over her daily adventures and discoveries.

They'd returned from a nice dinner, guests of an Javanese businessman and his wife, and they were sitting on the sofa examining a furniture catalog Kim had brought home from one of the rattan factories she had visited that day. It was a trial of sorts to sit so close to him and pretend that all she was doing was studying pictures of tables and chairs and discussing their various merits.

"You were talking about sharing innermost feelings," Sam reminded her. "How you don't know what I'm thinking."

"Oh, yes." That she remembered.

Sam closed the catalog and placed it on the coffee table. "So tell me your innermost feelings," he urged, leaning back against the sofa cushions and looking at her expectantly.

She shrugged. "You're not interested. You're just playing a game with me." It took an effort to be casual, to sound casual.

He took her hand and drew a little closer. "Oh, I'm interested."

She tried to ignore the feel of his hand, the tone of his voice, the terrible things they did to her blood. She wanted a cool head, a cool heart. "All right," she said breezily. "What subject did you have in mind? Politics, the stock market, the destruction of the rain forests?"

His eyes gazed into hers for a silent moment. "How about us?" he suggested.

"Us?"

"Yes, as in you and me. Tell me your innermost feelings about us."

She laughed. "We're an absurd marital experiment. I've told you before."

He stroked her hand. "Fair enough. What are your innermost feelings about me?"

Her heart made a nervous leap, and then, from somewhere came the voice of a little devil, taunting her. *So tell him!* it urged.

She slipped her hand out of his and took a deep breath, pushing aside warnings. "All right, I'll tell you. I remember very clearly how I felt about you eleven years ago, with all my silly little girl emotions." She forced herself to look right into his eyes. "When I saw you again in New York, the memory of it all came rushing back, and…" She paused and gave a long-suffering sigh. "And now I don't seem to be able to get rid of those feelings, the memories. They keep hanging around and I don't want them. I mean, it makes no sense to still feel this way. I'm…attracted to you and I can't imagine why."

One brow arched. "You're attracted to me and you can't imagine why. Now there's something a man loves to hear." His voice was dry. His hand was now playing with her hair, twisting a curl around his finger. He was sitting too close. She felt the warmth of his body, smelled the clean, male scent of him. Any minute now she was going to disintegrate. She had to stay calm. She could not allow him to think that all he had to do was touch her and she was putty. Not that it wasn't the truth, but she didn't want him to know.

Gathering composure, she manufactured a sunny smile. "Oh, your ego can take it," she said lightly. "Besides, you asked for it. You wanted my feelings, and you got them."

"So I did." His hand had crept up under her hair and played teasingly with her right earlobe. "So what do you intend to do with these unwanted amorous feelings you have for me?"

"I'm hoping they'll take care of themselves," she said casually, moving her head to get rid of his teasing hand. She was having a hard time breathing. "Die a natural death, so to speak," she sputtered desperately. He was stroking the back of her neck now. "A few more weeks under the same roof with you and I'll be cured, no doubt." Oh, Lord, she hoped so.

"Probably," he murmured, moving his face closer to hers again.

"Don't worry about it at all," she said reassuringly, fighting for lightness. "I won't throw myself at you again."

"Ah, a pity." His mouth was next to hers. "It could be fun, now that you're not a silly teenager anymore."

Heart pounding, she managed to twist her face away from his roving mouth. She had to be out of her mind, sitting here with him, allowing him to seduce her so blatantly. Trapped in the corner of the sofa, she could not get away from him, not unless she gave him a good shove, got to her feet and made a dash to safer territory. She didn't have the strength. Really she didn't.

"You're taking advantage of my feelings for you," she said, trying to sound cool, but her voice was trembling.

"The term 'taking advantage of' is rather negative. Would you like to know my innermost feelings about you?"

She felt mesmerized by his eyes, his low, warm voice. "You told me you think I'm amusing," she said, trying to keep her wits about her. "Like I'm a cute little child or something."

"You're most definitely not a cute little child." His

mouth was on hers, lightly touching, teasing. "You're a very sexy woman and you're driving me crazy."

"Why?" Her voice was faint for lack of air.

"Why?" The question seemed to surprise him.

She drew in a deep breath. "You need someone elegant and sophisticated and brainy. I'm not right for you."

He laughed softly. "Somebody sophisticated and brainy wouldn't drive me crazy. You do."

She sighed. "I don't know why."

"For a hundred reasons. Because you are who you are. How can I analyze that? You said you're attracted to me, even though you don't want to be. Why is that?"

"Because I'm stupid," she muttered.

Giving up all pretense at subtlety, he took her face in his hands and gave her a soul-shattering kiss, his mouth hot on hers, his tongue tormenting hers with promise.

Fire, passion. It was all there. Heat rushed through her and hunger filled her, swept her away. All her senses clamored for more.

He released her abruptly and a little moan of protest escaped her. His eyes were stormy black as they looked at her, searching for something in the depths of her eyes. "Tell me what's stupid about that," he demanded, his voice rough and unsteady.

She had no answer. She had no breath left to talk.

"And now," he said, stalking to the door to his room, "I'm going to have a very cold shower."

CHAPTER SIX

FOR the next two days Sam made no further seductive overtures. He did not kiss her, touch her or even give her amorous looks.

She should have been relieved.

Instead the memory of his kiss haunted her. Just thinking about it made her heart race.

Kim lay in bed in the dim light of dawn, thinking about Sam. She was always thinking about him.

She'd been fooling herself, pretending that what she was feeling was nothing but a superficial attraction, something that would go away once she'd spent time with him under the same roof.

It wasn't going away.

It was only getting stronger.

Every time they where together, the vibrations between them were undeniable. Why was she so drawn to this man? It was more than shallow physical attraction, she was sure about that. It was more than the memory of her teenage crush and the sheikh fantasies she had woven around him.

It was something deeper, something more real. She closed her eyes and sighed. Why analyze it? She wasn't good at that anyway. Why not simply accept that she was drawn to him on an instinctive level, that something deep inside her was connecting with something deep inside him. It was fate, destiny, that they should be together. A sweet mystery that she was not meant to understand.

It sounded so romantic, she smiled to herself.

So say it, a voice whispered from somewhere. *Say it, Kim.*

The light was growing brighter. Birds chirped their morning symphony in the guava tree outside her window.

Say it!

With a moan Kim pulled the sheet over her face. She closed her eyes and saw Sam's face in her mind's eye—the familiar quirky smile, the mysterious brooding in his eyes.

"I love him," she whispered.

That same afternoon she found the perfect house.

It was an omen, she was sure.

Eager to share the news immediately, she barged unannounced into Sam's private office, to the undisguised annoyance of his gorgeous Indonesian secretary.

"I think I've found the house!" she burst out, barely able to contain her excitement. "It's great, Sam! It has absolutely everything you want!" She was standing in front of his massive, immaculate desk, waving her hands to help her talk. "A great living room and a really nice study and a huge veranda with a spectacular view of the town! And it's empty! Ready to move in! Can you believe that?" She took in a gulp of air. "Let's go and look now. I can't wait for you to see it."

He regarded her with patient humor. "Are you quite sure you like this place?" he asked wryly.

"Yes, I do! And you will, too, Sam, I just know. Please, let's go and look now, while it's still light."

A few minutes later they walked out of the office together, past the irritated secretary who now had to cancel a meeting at the last minute, and Kim, victorious, couldn't resist giving her a triumphant smile.

The car was parked in front of the building, the driver holding open the door for them.

"So," said Sam as they settled themselves in the back seat. "This is the perfect house."

"Yes," she said, and grinned. "Except for the garden. It was left to its own devices for some time now and it's a tropical jungle, but that can be fixed. I've already found a gardener to hire."

Sam had told her he wanted a house that was spacious but homey. He needed a study, and plenty of room for entertaining and several rooms for overnight guests, yet not a mansion that required a map to find your way around. She'd looked at close to twenty houses, and the moment she had seen this one, she knew it was just right.

And Sam agreed. They wandered through the empty rooms, Kim pointing out the wonderful light, the newly painted walls, the modern bathrooms. He told her the house was just what he had in mind, perfect indeed. She felt a glow of pride. She told him how homey it would be with the right kind of furniture, how much space there was for guests and how the covered veranda could be furnished and used as an outside room. He said he thought it was an excellent idea and no doubt she would do a superb job doing just that. She enthused about the closet space, the wonderful kitchen, the lovely entryway.

She was gushing, she knew, but couldn't help herself. She was on a high, intoxicated by success, by Sam's praise. Intoxicated by Sam himself, by his presence, that mysterious, undeniable magnetism that drew her to him inexorably.

They stood at the veranda railing, admiring the view. The sun stood low in the sky and the heat of the day was subsiding.

"I'm sorry," Kim said, "I'm going on and on. Why don't you just tell me to stop jabbering?" She was telling him things he was perfectly capable of seeing for himself.

One corner of his mouth lifted in amusement. "I like

your enthusiasm, Kim.'' He covered her hand with his
and glanced down at her with a smile. ''It's a wonderful
house and you did a great job finding it in such a short
time.''

His praise gave her a new thrill. ''It was fun,'' she
said. ''And Maya was a great help.'' She glanced down
at his strong brown hand on top of hers on the railing.
It was the first time he'd touched her since that devas-
tating kiss a few days ago. She gazed at it, feeling herself
react, feeling the quickening of her pulse, the familiar
tingling all over. Her breathing was growing shallower
and she was suddenly afraid to look at him. A silence
hung between them, electric, expectant. A bird chirped
in the mango tree, a liquid, warbling sound. The warm
breeze lifted a curl away from her cheek. Every cell of
her body seemed alive, quivering, waiting.

He caught her chin in his big hand and gently lifted
her face to his. His eyes gleamed with dark, coppery
flames, and her heart lurched as she saw the heat in
them. She lowered her gaze. His mouth was close, so
close. She wanted him to kiss her, wanted it with a deep,
aching longing. She waited, trembling, watching his
mouth.

''Are you cured yet?'' he asked in a low voice.

''Cured?'' It was a mere whisper. Her gaze flew up
to meet his eyes. Her heart throbbed and she had trouble
dragging air into her lungs.

''Cured of your attraction for me.''

And then he kissed her and she knew she wasn't cured
at all.

It was the most wonderful, exhilarating feeling, the
heat rushing through her, the dizzy dancing in her
head—who would want to be cured of that?

He had wrapped his arms around her, holding her
against him in an intimate embrace. His mouth took hers

without qualm or hesitation, his tongue seducing hers into an erotic dance of desire.

She felt deliciously reckless as she yielded to him, felt the tension mounting between them.

His hands stroked her back, restlessly, slipped under her short little top and settled warm against her bare skin. Oh, it felt good, so good. She wanted more, she wanted—

A muted ringing insinuated itself into the magic bubble surrounding them. Sam drew back from her with a soft groan of frustration. Eyes closed, he reached blindly for his jacket hanging over the railing and retrieved the cell phone from one of the pockets.

Kim leaned weakly against the railing, feeling bereft. She watched the dark frown on Sam's face, heard the short, clipped tone of his voice. A crisis at the office, she surmised from his end of the conversation. Probably his secretary calling. She wrapped her arms around herself as if to hold herself together. Her body felt dangerously boneless.

A moment later Sam flipped the phone off, slipped it back into his pocket and flung the jacket over his shoulder.

"We'd better go," he said, all business again. She felt a moment of resentment to know he'd so easily found himself in another mode, the kiss forgotten, shoved aside for more important matters.

She nodded. "All right." Straightening away from the support of the railing, she hoped her legs would hold her up. Sagging to the ground as if she were a limp rag doll would not do wonders for her dignity. Fortunately she managed to stay upright, be it a shade unsteady.

"I'll drop you off at the hotel," Sam said, glancing at his watch. "I have to go back to the office to take care of a few things, but I shouldn't be too long." He frowned as if suddenly remembering something. "What time are we expected at Joel and Maya's?"

They'd been invited to dinner and she'd been looking forward to it, but now she suddenly wished that they didn't have to go. She didn't want to go anywhere at all. She wanted to go back to the hotel with Sam. She wanted him to finish what he had started. She wanted to be back in that magic bubble with him.

"Seven."

He nodded. "No problem." His gaze lingered on her face and a slow smile slipped around his mouth and into his eyes. "Hey," he said softly, "I like the way you kiss."

Her heart lurched. "How's that?" she asked before she could stop herself. Oh, God, she was such an idiot.

He chuckled. "You kiss like you really mean it."

She dragged in a fortifying breath of air, trying for a bit of frivolity. She made a dismissive gesture. "Actually I was just faking." She slipped through the double doors into the empty living room, hearing Sam's laugh behind her. She liked the deep, rich sound of it, and wished she could make him laugh more often.

Kim had finished showering, dressing and adorning herself, and settled herself on the sofa with a book to wait for Sam. She'd put on a slinky little silk dress—short, passionate red and sexy. It wasn't what she'd wear to a restaurant, a business reception or some other formal affair, but Maya would only approve and most likely would have slithered into something rather seductive herself.

She heard the key in the door before she'd even read a page and Sam strode in, carrying a mass of red roses.

Kim's heart did a somersault. Red roses!

"I thought a little floral thank-you was in order," Sam

said with a touch of humor in his voice. Kim leaped to her feet and took the proffered flowers from him.

"Thank you for what?" she asked.

"Thank you for being here, for finding me a house and for everything you're doing," he said.

Her heart made another little flip. The fragrance of the roses permeated the air. "They're gorgeous," she said, feeling suddenly shy, like a teenager. Red roses. From Sam. She tried not to read too much into it. Tried, but failed.

He was observing her, a faint smile quirking the corners of his mouth. "Woman in red," he said. "I should take a picture of you. The color of the flowers matches your dress."

"Yes, I guess they do." She couldn't tear her gaze away from him.

"You look very...alluring," Sam said, and she caught the devilish gleam in his eyes.

She attempted to look demure and lowered her gaze to the flowers in her arms. "I felt inspired," she said, a delicious thrill going down her back at the flirtatiousness of her reply.

He gave a soft laugh.

She scooted over to the phone. "I'll call housekeeping and get a vase to put them in," she said before he could answer.

All during dinner she kept feeling a delicious sense of anticipation as she thought of Sam's kiss, the roses, the glitter of desire in his eyes as he watched her from across the table.

Every bite of food was wonderful. Every glance from Sam made her blood sing. For dessert, Maya had created tiramisu. How she'd managed to get all the ingredients, Kim had no idea, but it was heavenly delicious.

"I think," said Maya, "that tiramisu is the absolute most sensuous, sexiest dessert in the world."

"I never thought of a dessert in those terms," said Joel, who had a more mundane view of food, as fuel for the body.

"It's Italian," Kim said, as if that explained everything. Floating in a heightened state of romantic awareness, she could well understand Maya's sentiments about the taste-titillating confection.

"I'll explain it to you," Maya said generously.

"I can't wait." Joel rolled his eyes.

Maya spooned a bite of the dessert, savored it with her eyes closed and gave a sort of swooning sigh. "First you have the rich, sweet rapture of the mascarpone," she said in a low, seductive voice, pausing to give everyone a chance to imagine it. "Then there's the tantalizing whisper of chocolate." She ran her tongue around her lips. "Then comes the dark passion of espresso coffee, and the intoxicating delight of the Amaretto." She looked around the table meaningfully. "All of it wrapped into one tempting confection. "Perfection, wouldn't you agree?"

"Now I understand why she married me," said Joel, grinning. "I'm her tiramisu."

After coffee, Kim and Sam took their leave. Entering the suite, the scent of roses greeted them, as well as, magically, the sight of a full moon shining in through the window.

He'd barely closed the door behind him before Sam caught her into his arms and kissed her; kissed her with such tender passion that she was instantly swept away on a wave of delirious longing.

Such sweet magic. A soft little moan escaped her.

"You never answered my question," he whispered against her lips.

Her legs could barely hold her up, and she was leaning

against his hard chest for support. Her head was spinning and she couldn't manufacture a coherent thought to save her life.

"What question?" she murmured.

"Are you cured? Of your attraction for me?"

She let out a languid sigh. "Let me think."

He gave a low rumble of a laugh, swept her right off her feet and carried her into her bedroom as if she weighed nothing at all. "I'll help you think," he offered generously.

"Thank you," she muttered automatically, dizzily aware of the warm scent of his skin, aware that she wanted him more than she wanted anything in the world.

She clung to him as he released his hold around her legs and gently set her on her feet. Leaning into him, she felt the whole hard length of his body against hers, felt his warmth against her thighs and belly and breasts. He held her quietly for a long, long moment, his heart thudding as loud as hers. He combed his fingers through her hair, over and over, and she'd never known how exquisitely sensual the caress could be.

His hands slipped to her back, reaching for the zipper of her dress, then sliding it down slowly, very slowly. Gently he eased away from her a little to allow the dress to slip down her body and fall around her ankles in a pool of shimmery red silk. The room glowed in the silver light of the moon and she watched his eyes sliding over her as she stood in front of him in her red bra and panties, and for an instant she felt an overwhelming vulnerability and an unfamiliar shyness. The feeling got swallowed up as he kissed her, not slowly or gently, but with a sudden hot hunger that set her blood on fire. Then, with an effort, he abruptly drew away, leaving only his hands on her shoulders.

"Kim," he said, his voice husky, "if you don't want this, you'd better tell me now."

She felt a wave of sweetness. Her body trembled, ached for him. She shook her head, leaned back into him, needing his closeness. "Please make love to me, Sam," she whispered. "I've been thinking about it all evening."

He caught her up in his arms with a groan. "So have I," he muttered and lowered her onto the bed. He leaned over her, his face close to hers, "And don't worry about a thing," he said softly, "I'll take care of you." He straightened and stripped off his clothes with uncharacteristic carelessness.

Washed in moonlight, the sight of him, naked and aroused, took her breath away. Then he was on the bed with her, stroking her with his hands and mouth as he took off her bra and panties...and she sighed, drawing him to her, over her, holding him tight, wanting to feel all of him, his warmth, his strength, his skin against hers.

"You feel so good," he whispered. "So good." He shifted lower to gain access to her breasts and he teased the nipples with his mouth and tongue, sweet torture that flooded her with intoxicating heat.

His hands and mouth explored her body, finding all the sensitive, secret places, sending delicious tremors through her. And it was magic giving back what she received, moving her hands over his body, teasing, stroking, kissing him with all the power of her own passion. And then all was breathless abandon as she felt herself being swept up and up into dizzy heights of sensation, the tension exquisite, unbearable, her body throbbing with it.

"Kim?" His voice was barely a whisper. She gave a soft gasp in answer and they tumbled over the edge together, trembling and clinging feverishly to each other—falling, falling until finally the turbulence stilled and they lay spent in each other's arms.

It took a while for her heart to find its normal rhythm

again. Her face on his chest, Kim reveled in the feeling of the sweet languor stealing over her. She rubbed her cheek softly against him, feeling the springy hair tickling her nose. Nothing could be more wonderful than this, she thought dreamily.

"You're very quiet," he whispered.

She smiled into the darkness. "Sometimes even I have no words," she whispered back and he laughed softly, stroking the back of her head.

"Where were you all this time?" he asked.

"In New York, meeting all the wrong men." She sighed contentedly, and tried to snuggle even closer to him, but it wasn't possible. They fell quiet again and after a while she wondered if he had fallen asleep.

"Sam?" she whispered.

"Mmm?"

"I thought you were asleep."

"No, I'm just lying here savoring the feel of you in my arms."

She smiled again. "I'm glad you enjoy it."

"Mmm. I do, very much."

She reached up and traced a finger around his mouth. "Tell me, what is your favorite dessert?"

She heard his surprised chuckle. *"What?"*

"What is your favorite dessert? Ice cream, apple pie, cheese cake?"

"Tiramisu, of course."

"Mine, too." She lifted her head and brushed her lips across his. "I was just thinking," she whispered, "that this was even better than tiramisu."

For days Kim floated on the proverbial clouds, reveling in the joy of loving Sam. They laughed, they kissed, they made wonderful, passionate love. She'd never known how magical it could be. She practically danced through the days, shopping for household appliances and kitchen equipment and doing a hundred other housewifely things, like the perfect homemaker in some incredibly corny television commercial from the fifties.

At the end of the day she'd get dressed for dinner and wait breathlessly for Sam to come through the door so she could fling herself into his arms.

Everything was working out beautifully. The house was bought, a gardener hired, furniture selected, all in record time.

Like a dutiful wife, Kim was working diligently on developing their social life, which was also an important part of settling successfully in a new place—at least in her opinion. Maya had generously drawn her into her circle of friends and it had taken little time for Kim to connect with a number of kindred spirits. Sam, she discovered, had some hermit tendencies, but once out he always enjoyed himself. They were often out in the evenings, invited to parties, to dinner, for drinks. Because of Sam's work, cocktail parties and receptions and business dinners were on the program as well.

One day they were invited for a weekend stay the following month in Sarangan, a cool resort town high in the mountains in the western part of the island. The invitation had come from one of Sam's Indonesian business acquaintances and his American wife, Joanna, who owned a villa in the town.

"Sarangan?" Kim asked. "Sarangan is great, Sam! I remember being there when I was a kid. At night it's *cold* up there!" She laughed. "It's amazing!"

Sarangan was a good place to mix business with pleasure, Sam told her, and apparently some business had to be conducted. To this end, another businessman and his wife were invited as well.

"You need a break," said Sam. "You'll enjoy a little diversion."

"I don't need a break, but I'll enjoy it anyway," said

Kim. She was looking forward to the weekend, to spending some lazy time and breathing in some cool, bracing mountain air.

One steamy afternoon the furniture was delivered to the empty house and Kim was surveying the chairs, tables and sofas haphazardly deposited in the middle of the living room, trying to arrange them in her mind before doing it for real. Some help would be nice, she concluded…some strong manly muscles to— Her thoughts were interrupted by sounds coming from the front of the house.

"Hello?" a deep male voice called out. "Anybody home?"

She scooted across the room to the hall, finding the front door open and a tall blond man in tennis clothes standing just inside with his hand on the doorknob. A man with muscles, no less. Had she manifested him? She almost laughed.

"Hi," he said. "The door was open. I knocked but got no answer." He spoke with an American accent, a faint Southern twang.

"Hi," she said. "I guess I didn't hear you." He was lean and good-looking and very tanned, like someone who spent a lot of time outdoors. She'd seen him a couple of times, jogging in the late afternoon, and he'd waved at her then, but she'd not spoken to him before.

"Just wanted to introduce myself," he said with a friendly grin. "I live next door. Actually I live in New York, but my parents live next door and I'm visiting them while I'm on assignment here." He held out a tanned hand. "I'm Nick Harrison."

His grip was firm and warm. Laughter lines fanned from the corners of his blue eyes and she guessed him to be in his middle thirties. She smiled back at him. "I'm Kim Rasheed." How easy the lie was.

"I saw the furniture being delivered a little while ago," he commented. "Just moving in?"

She nodded. "Trying to decide where to put it."

"You need any help? Shoving and pushing, I mean?"

She grinned and stepped back from the door to allow him entrance. "Come right on in...your timing is perfect." She closed the door behind him. "May I offer you something cold to drink?" A new fridge was humming away in the kitchen stocked with some drinks and snacks to keep her going during the day.

Nick was a photojournalist, he told her as they maneuvered sofas and tables. He was doing an extensive, multipart article on the island of Java, its culture and people and scenery. As they worked, he amused her with his stories.

Two hours later the living room furniture was arranged the way she wanted it; the beds in the bedrooms had been assembled after Nick had gone home to raid his father's toolbox. His mother then invited her to come over for some iced tea, to relax for a bit and to get to know each other.

So, by the end of the afternoon a lot of work had been completed, and Kim had made friends with the neighbors. After all, that, too, was an important part of making a home in a new place.

With Maya's help, she'd done massive amounts of shopping, stocking the kitchen with pots and pans, coffeemaker, food processor, mixer and a myriad of other cooking utensils. Everything was neat and clean and in order. She was putting away the last of the storage containers on a shelf, singing a sappy old classic about being in love and feeling on top of the mountain and the world being a magical place, humming part of it because she didn't know all the words. But the tune was wonderful, one that stuck in your mind and haunted you all day and followed you into your dreams.

She became aware suddenly of a tingling feeling all over, a sense that she was not alone. Turning her head, she discovered Sam leaning lazily against the door frame, hands in his pockets, watching her with a smile tugging at his mouth. By the looks of it he'd been there for some time.

"How long have you been standing there?" she asked suspiciously, coming down from the step stool.

"A while." His smile deepened. "I didn't want to disrupt your performance."

"My singing is not meant to be heard by anyone but myself." She feigned a cool look. She didn't feel cool; not looking at him, ever. He was wearing office clothes, suit trousers, shirt and tie, but no jacket.

He moved toward her and reached out to capture a loose curl and slowly wound it around his finger, bringing her face closer to his. "Very selfish of you. I quite enjoyed it."

"It's not good manners to watch someone when they're not aware of it," she said loftily, feeling warmth begin to spread through her. "Very voyeuristic. I didn't know this side of you, Samiir."

"It only comes out when I'm with you." He released the curl and caught her face between his hands. His eyes gleamed darkly into hers. "I like watching you," he said softly.

She closed her eyes and felt his mouth on hers, teasing, taunting. "Why are you here?" she whispered, feeling desire unfurling inside her.

"Because I want you."

Her pulse quickened at the simple statement. *Because I want you.* Wonderful, sexy words that made her blood sing. "In the middle of a working day? Just like that?"

"Yes, just like that." He scooped her up in his arms,

carried her into the living room and lowered her gently onto the silk Chinese rug she'd bought two days ago.

He sat down next to her, and started working the small buttons on her red cotton top. "I was in the middle of a meeting," he said, "thinking about you."

She tried to visualize it: Sam in his immaculate suit at a shiny conference table surrounded by other dignified businesspeople discussing Important Decisions and Crucial Matters, while Sam secretly fantasized about her.

"In the middle of a meeting?" She couldn't believe she was having such a distracting influence on Samiir Rasheed, the self-composed man in utter control of his emotions. He slipped the little shirt off her shoulders, down her arms, his dark gaze meeting hers.

"In the middle of an important meeting with some government hotshots from Jakarta discussing licensing agreements."

"Very important," she murmured, feeling his hands get rid of her bra with swift, expertise movements.

"Very important," he agreed, stroking her bare breasts. "And all I could think of was you. Here, in this house, all by yourself."

"I'm a danger to the welfare of your company," she said, her breath growing shallow.

"You've bewitched me. You've got me under your spell," he murmured as he continued fondling her.

Her breasts felt full and warm with his touch. "So, what did you do?"

"I left." He lowered his mouth and kissed first one, then the other nipple.

"You left the meeting?" It was difficult to talk, to think.

"In the middle of it."

She felt a thrill of excitement. She laughed softly. "It has a delicious illicit ring about it. I wonder what that proper secretary of yours was thinking."

"I didn't feel the need to explain it to her," he said wryly, "and I don't care in the least what she might be thinking."

He stripped off his clothes with amazing speed while she worked herself out of the rest of hers, amazed at the suddenness with which he had set her aflame. He wanted her, and it seemed like the sexiest thing in the world to think of him dropping everything and rushing over to make love with her here in this house.

The silk rug was soft against her skin, Sam's mouth hot and urgent on hers. No need for finesse, no need for long, delicate play. Just this, the wildness between them, the primal need for fulfillment. All she was aware of was his mouth and hands and body, hungry for her, touching and tasting until the wild abandon of her own body's responses left her mindless in the storm that followed.

Afterward they clutched each other breathlessly, their bodies damp, their hearts pounding.

Finally, calmness and sanity restored, he kissed her softly. "I'm so glad you didn't have a headache," he said.

She laughed. "Me, too."

She did have a headache the next afternoon, a heavy throbbing in her head that seemed to mimic the weather outside. The sky loomed dark and ominous, the air was thick and damp—a tropical downpour in the making.

Kim seldom had headaches and she didn't like this one. It wasn't fair, and she had not a clue as to what might have caused it. She was having such a great day. In the morning she'd gone to the plant and flower market and bought several carloads of greenery for the house and veranda, haggling and joking good-naturedly with the vendors. She loved the markets, loved the busyness and color and fun.

She'd spent the afternoon repotting the plants into decorative containers and arranging them in the various places that called out for foliage. It transformed the rooms, gave them life and an atmosphere of cool, green airiness. The veranda looked like a lovely garden room, something straight out of a glossy magazine.

It was four o'clock now and the world lay shrouded in a gloomy darkness. Normally she found it exciting, this stark contrast with the radiant tropical sunshine that had bathed the world only half an hour earlier. She liked the drama of a sudden rainfall, the passion of a really good deluge. It would be over as suddenly as it had started and the sun would come out again and the world would gleam and drip with freshness.

She felt no excitement now, only an unfamiliar, brooding apprehension. Her head throbbed, her heart felt strangely heavy. She wanted to get out of the house and get back to the hotel before the world would be awash in water. She barely made it.

In the room she found a note from Sam saying something had come up and he was unable to make it for dinner tonight and that he would probably be late coming back.

She sighed, disappointed and relieved at the same time. What she really felt like doing was having a bath, putting on her bathrobe and ordering some food from room service. Maybe there was a good movie on television, or maybe she'd simply crawl into bed with a good book. Good grief, what was the matter with her? She couldn't remember the last time she had felt this way—it wasn't like her to feel so gloomy and listless for no reason at all.

It was after midnight when she finally heard Sam come into the sitting room. She'd dozed off and on, unable to really fall asleep, her mind restless and uneasy.

She slipped out of bed, put on her kimono and made her way into the sitting room.

Sam stood at the window, staring out into the darkness. His jacket lay on a nearby chair. She noticed the rigid stance of his body, the taut line of his shoulders under the white dress shirt. An unaccountable apprehension slithered through her.

"Sam?" she asked softly, hearing the concern in her voice.

He turned to look at her. "I thought you'd be in bed," he said, his voice without inflection. He'd loosened his tie and unbuttoned the collar of his shirt. He looked exhausted, his eyes full of dark shadows.

"You look tired," she said, moving closer. "Problems?"

"I'm handling it," he said tonelessly. There was something odd about his expression, the tone of his voice—something cold and angry that was controlled with utmost effort. An awful sense of foreboding gripped her. She put her arms around his neck.

"Is something wrong?"

He held her briefly, with one arm, then released her. "Nothing that can't be worked out," he said, and with a sickening feeling she sensed him withdraw from her, saw the shuttered look in his eyes.

Her throat tightened painfully. "Sam, please," she whispered, her heart drumming with anxiety.

"Better go to sleep, Kim," he said wearily. "I'll be up for a while."

Instinctively she knew not to press further, but it took a lot of effort to simply drop the matter then and there, to leave him alone, and go back to her room.

As she lay in bed, her heart heavy with dread, she heard him pace, heard the rustling of papers and the clicking of his notebook keyboard. Was he working? Then she heard him talk, and she realized he must be on the phone since she registered no answering voice. Words floated in through the closed door, unfamiliar sounds, incomprehensible. After a few moments it dawned on her that it wasn't English that she was hearing. It must be Arabic. Was he talking to his uncle in New York? To family members in Jordan? She closed her eyes and sighed, wishing she'd just fall sleep and find a reprieve from her mind wanderings.

Finally, hours later it seemed, she heard the opening of a door, the door into Sam's bedroom. Then all went quiet.

Her stomach churned. He'd not come to sleep with her in her bed. He'd gone to his own bed, where he hadn't slept for two weeks. Fear crawled through her.

You're an idiot, she said to herself. He thinks you're asleep; he's being considerate, not wanting to wake you. That's all it is.

But she knew it wasn't. She'd seen the withdrawal in his eyes, the emotional distancing. Something was very wrong.

He didn't talk about the trouble, not the next day, not the day after that. She sensed in him a terrible, brooding anger that frightened her. When she tried to talk to him, asked him what the problem was, he was detached and uncommunicative, saying only that he didn't mean to hurt her feelings, but that the problem he was dealing with required all his time and attention. She asked if there was anything she could do to help. No, he said, there was nothing, but he appreciated the offer. She fell victim to a mixture of emotions—anger, rejection, helplessness, despair. At times she felt the wild urge to shout at him, shake him, tell him she wanted him back, wanted back the Sam who was lost to her now. But seeing the implacable look in his eyes, the cool distance in his expression, she knew it would do no good. He had retreated to a lonely inner space where she could not reach him, where he allowed her no entrance.

A week went by. Then another. Sam came home late every night, slept in his own bed every night. Then one day he packed a bag and left for a business trip to New York.

Overnight he had become a stranger.

Sam sat on the edge of the bed in the Rasheed New York apartment and stared at the telephone, fighting the impulse to reach for it and call Kim.

He'd been in a state of shocked rage for the last two weeks and the only way he had been able to hold it together had been to block everything out and focus on the crisis at hand. Not to allow anything else to sap his energy and concentration. Not to allow anyone to come near him.

Not even Kim.

He could not confide in her, tell her why he was here. He could not bear to see the doubt and suspicion in her eyes. Or worse, contempt.

He did not want to lose her.

He stared at the telephone, feeling the ache in his gut. He wanted to hear her voice, he wanted to hear her laughter.

With a vicious curse and a violent swipe of his arm, he sent the phone flying off the bedside table and crashing onto the floor.

CHAPTER SEVEN

"YOU'RE pushing me away," she said to the door of Sam's empty bedroom. The quiet hotel suite was getting on her nerves and now and again she found herself talking out loud addressing the absent Sam: "You want to know my innermost feelings? Let me tell you my innermost feelings. I feel like a one-night stand you dropped like a hot brick. I feel insulted and I feel betrayed. And now that I'm on a roll, let me tell you that I think you are an arrogant swine and I hate it that you treated me like some cheap floozy."

Her ravings didn't make her feel better. She flopped down on the sofa and wept.

After that she would start in on herself, telling herself in unflattering terms that she was seriously lacking in intelligence to have gotten herself in this situation. After all, she'd been right there with her eyes wide-open. She'd allowed herself to fall for the wrong man once again, allowed herself to dream and be happy and hopeful. She'd been a romantic fool to fall for a man like Sam. He didn't want her in his life. He didn't want to share his problems. She couldn't live with a man like that. She should have known better. She should have been smarter.

And so on and so forth.

After wallowing in self-pity for a while she decided she wasn't going to allow him to make her so miserable; she couldn't allow him to have so much power. She'd made a mistake, a serious one, but she was not going to let him know how hurt she was; she had, after all, her pride. And she would try to keep her dignity.

101

She would finish the job she was hired to do, and do it well. She would be professional and polite, and try to be cheerful for her own benefit. All during the next few days she gave herself pep talks, breaking down into tears at intervals, but generally feeling stronger little by little.

Then Sam returned from New York and the moment he strode through the door and she saw his familiar face something inside her ignited and her knees turned weak.

It wasn't fair. It really wasn't.

For a frozen moment she simply stared at him, filling herself with the sight of him, the dark, compelling eyes, the strong-jawed face, the broad chest that felt so good under her cheek. She felt the sweet, familiar hunger stirring deep inside her and fought the urge to throw her arms around him and hold him close against her. Tell him she loved him.

No, you don't!

"Hi," she said, forging a smile, hoping he didn't notice her shaking knees and trembling voice. Her mind was a tangled mess of conflicting emotions and she fought a panicky urge to run—from him, from herself.

"Hello, Kim." He looked at her intently, but his eyes were unreadable and his face gave nothing away.

She struggled for composure. "I was just on my way out," she said, which was the truth. "Is there anything you need me to do?" To her relief she managed to sound calm.

"No," he said, "thank you."

"Then I'm off." She scooped up her purse and breezed toward the door.

"Wait," he said, raking a tired hand through his hair. "Will you be back for dinner?"

She shook her head. "I'm having dinner with friends." With the Harrisons, actually, Nick and his parents. "I didn't know you would be back today."

"I should have let you know, I'm sorry."

"Doesn't matter at all," she said lightly. "We do need to talk, though, soon. I have some questions about the servants you'd like me to hire and a few other things concerning the house."

He nodded. "Of course."

"See you later then." She dashed out, closing the door behind her.

Outside, she took in a deep, shaky breath. Oh, Lord, it wasn't going to be easy.

It was late when she finally made her way back to the hotel. In spite of her thoughts of Sam, it had been a nice evening with good food and interesting people. She put the key in the door and took in a deep breath, steeling herself before going in.

Sam was sitting on the sofa wearing jeans and a black T-shirt, all casual male appeal. A stack of papers was perched on his thighs and his feet were bare.

"Hi," she said sunnily. "Thought you'd be asleep."

"I woke up."

"Jet lag, what a drag," she sympathized, flinging her purse onto a chair. She had vowed to be cheerful and pleasant in dealing with Sam and she would try if it killed her.

"How was your dinner?" he asked.

"Nice, real nice." She wiped a strand of hair behind her ear. "So, how was your trip?"

"Hell," he said. "How's everything coming with the house?"

"Oh, fine." She made a casual gesture with her hand. "Come have a look, anytime." He was watching her and she flashed him another breezy smile. "You'll be able to move in soon."

He motioned to a chair. "Sit down," he suggested.

"Good idea." She plunked herself down in one of the

chairs and crossed her legs. "So, tell me about your trip. Hell sounds pretty bad."

"I've had more fun at the dentist," he said dryly. He gave her a searching look. "I think I owe you an apology, Kim."

"An apology?" she echoed. "What for?" She was not in the mood to be serious. She was tired of being sad and serious. It was so much more fun to be happy. And she was determined to be happy. She swung her right leg back and forth, her high-heeled sandal dangling from her big toe, swaying gently.

"I didn't do the right thing by you these last few weeks. I didn't treat you well and I am sorry."

How right he was. "Yes, well, I understand," she said airily. "Work before pleasure, of course. I didn't understand that immediately, never having had a fling with a workaholic before, but you know, it was nice while it lasted."

His jaw tensed and something flickered in his dark eyes. "I wasn't thinking it was a fling," he said, his voice a bit rough.

"Really? No, I guess I'm supposed to be your wife." She twisted the ring on her finger. "A game, that's what it was." She gave an exaggerated sigh. "And you played it so well that I didn't immediately realize it was all an act, silly me." She tossed her head back and laughed. "You told me once that I amused you. I was a play thing, wasn't I? And then when you got busy and buried yourself in all that work there was no more time for playing and you simply threw me out like a toy you didn't want anymore. I—"

The muscles in his face worked. "Stop it!" he said roughly. Coming to his feet, he stood looming over her.

She looked up at his dark face and widened her eyes in innocence. "Well, it's true, isn't it? I was just a diversion. I understand, you know. It's quite all right."

She yawned expansively. "I'd better go to bed, I'm tired."

His face was as hard as steel. "Stop the act, Kim," he growled.

"Act? Me? No, I think it's you, sir, who's been doing the acting, playing the amorous lover." She came to her feet and he stepped back to give her space, saying nothing. He stood there, just looking at her.

She smiled at him. "Good night, Sam."

He was silent, but in the moment before she swung away from him she caught a glimpse of some dark emotion in his eyes, something she couldn't quite read, something painful and secret struggling to come out.

Surely she was mistaken.

He was going to lose her. Sam stared at the closed door to Kim's room, desolation creeping into his every pore.

He'd never quite known what it was he wanted until Kim had sashayed back into his life, bringing with her the warmth and life and joy he had once found in her family when he was grieving for the loss of his own parents.

Her warmth and vibrancy had filled the dark, lonely spaces in his soul. He ached to hold her, to know the nightmare was over. Only the nightmare was not over and might not be for a long time.

Tell her, a little voice urged.

The thought of telling her struck terror in his soul. Would she trust him? Despise him? Would she leave?

Anger, hot and bitter, burned his throat.

He was going to lose her because of another woman.

"Tell me again why you didn't want to live in a furnished house, or a hotel room?" Kim asked Sam one night, her voice irritated and impatient. She'd tried in vain to get him to show interest in coming to an art gallery with her to look at some wonderful batik paintings she had discovered.

In the past few days, Kim had worked on the finishing touches of the house, hardly seeing Sam at all. Now and again, when she did have the dubious pleasure of his presence, she'd ask him questions as to what he liked and preferred, her manner cheerful but businesslike. He was courteous, but showed little or no interest, his mind somewhere else.

"Not now, Kim," he said impatiently, his gaze focused on a stack of paper.

She felt a surge of anger, anger she was trying hard not to show. She was sorry she'd taken the job and come with him to the other side of the world. She was trying hard and he didn't even care. He didn't care about her.

"Yes, now!" she said sharply. "I want to talk to you about this now!"

He frowned. "What is it?"

"Why are you doing this? Why are you suddenly acting as if you don't care anymore?" Why do you act as if you don't care about *me* anymore? She wanted to add, feeling her heart ache. But she didn't say the words out loud. Her pride wouldn't let her.

"It's only a house, Kim," he said tiredly. "It's only furniture, and paintings and things."

"You wanted a home! A place that feels like it's all yours, instead of this!" She made a sweeping gesture, encompassing the hotel sitting room, which was beautifully furnished but impersonal.

"I knew beforehand I wouldn't have time to take care of these things, Kim," he said with exaggerated patience. "That's why I wanted you to come, so you could take care of it all."

"Don't you want anything to do with it then? I mean, don't you even want to make some choices about the art you hang on your walls?"

"I trust your judgment, Kim."

She stared at him. "Much as that pleases me, it does not make sense that you don't want any say in it at all. It's your house, not mine, in the end."

He rubbed his neck. "I know," he said tonelessly. He closed his eyes briefly, as if he wanted to shut her out, shut out the world. "I'm sorry I'm not being more helpful, but I would appreciate it if you would bear with me for the time being. I'm swamped with work."

Swamped with work. There was something much more than the swamping of work going on and he didn't deceive her for a minute.

"What's going on, Sam? What is it you're not telling me?"

She caught the struggle in his eyes—hesitation, pain. For that one flash of a moment his face showed an uncharacteristic vulnerability and she almost reached out to him, her heart flooding with a tenderness, a need to comfort. The moment passed too quickly and next his face was as closed as a tomb, as if he were hiding in some impenetrable fortress.

"There are unexpected complications, Kim," he said tersely. "Business problems. It has nothing to do with you."

He was lying. She knew he was.

She looked straight into his eyes. "I see," she said coolly. "Well, I won't bother you anymore." She swung around and fled into her bedroom, resisting the urge to slam the door.

Well, if she couldn't please him, she could please herself. She kicked her shoes into a corner and began stripping off her clothes, fighting back hot tears of fury. She was simply not going to worry if something was to his taste anymore. She wouldn't bother him with questions. She'd simply go ahead and do what needed to be done and do it the way she liked it. It made no difference anyway. She could just pretend it was her own place and put it together for herself. The freedom would be wonderful.

She flopped herself on the bed, stared at the ceiling and wondered what he wasn't telling her. What had happened that night he had turned himself away from her?

"Is it straight?" Nick asked. He was standing on a ladder helping Kim to hang the large batik painting she'd bought that morning. It had a magnificent place in the living room on a large wall where it got all the attention.

"It's perfect," she said, stepping back and admiring the result. She'd bought the painting without Sam having seen it. She loved the bold, contemporary design of bamboo stalks and leaves set off against a dusky sky.

Nick stepped off the ladder and stood next to her, surveying the painting from a distance. "It's stunning, Kim," he said with admiration. "Excellent choice."

"Thanks." She turned and grinned at him, pleased with his praise—then she saw Sam standing in the doorway, watching them. Her heart made a painful little leap. "Sam," she said, and Nick turned and looked at Sam.

The two men had not met and Kim made the introductions. She could not bring herself to call Sam her husband, although she'd told Nick, as she'd told everyone else, that she was married. By the look in Sam's eyes, she could tell that her omission had not escaped him. His gaze settled on the painting, studying it.

"I like it," he said. "My wife has excellent taste," he added, looking at Nick.

Kim was aware of the tension in the air. Aware Sam was establishing territory, establishing his possession over her. She clenched her hands. How dare he? In private he acted as if he didn't want her and now, here, he pretended he was her devoted, admiring husband.

Nick nodded. "So she does." He gestured around the

room. "She's making something very special out of this house."

Sam nodded coolly.

"Nick has been very helpful," Kim said, unable to resist the temptation. "He helped me move the furniture around and put the bookcases and the beds together."

Nick made a dismissive gesture. "It was nothing. Anytime." He glanced at his watch. "I have to get going," he added before either one of them could say anything else. He made for the door, smiled, wished them *selamat malam* and was gone.

Kim wondered why Sam had come, but she didn't want to ask. She was sure it wasn't because he'd been fantasizing about her while in the middle of an important meeting. The memory slashed her like a knife. Hastily she bent over and scooped up some of the wrapping paper that had protected the painting and began to bundle it.

"Sounds like he's been hanging around the house quite a bit," Sam commented.

She didn't like the censure in his tone and suppressed a snappish comment with an effort.

"Oh," she said casually, "it's great having him to help me, and he's good company." Which was more than could be said of her so-called husband.

"Well, tell him to stay out of my house." Sam's voice was as cold as ice.

She couldn't believe what she was hearing and she almost gaped at him, but not quite. "I hope you're kidding," she said lightly.

He thrust his hands into his pockets. "We're expected at a cocktail party in an hour," he said, not responding to her comment. "I came to get you now so you'd have time to get ready."

A cocktail party. She liked parties, liked being with people, liked talking and laughing. What she didn't like was having to play the role of Sam's wife, not now, not anymore. But it was part of the job and she'd just have to manage the act for another night.

She nodded. "All right, but I'll need to leave a message for Tuki." Tuki was the driver and he was coming in an hour expecting to drive her back to the hotel.

"He was at the office. I told him I was picking you up and he could go home."

He began walking through the rooms, looking around, taking in all that she had done since the last time he'd been there, the time they'd made love on the Chinese rug. Her heart contracted painfully.

"You're doing a wonderful job," Sam said, looking at her with a hint of a smile. She hadn't seen him smile for a long time and she felt something shift in her, felt a longing for the man he had been not so long ago. The man who had enjoyed being with her, enjoyed laughing with her, enjoyed making love with her.

"Thank you," she said, and her voice sounded a little strange in her own ears. What happened to us, Sam? she was tempted to ask, but the words stayed unspoken in her mind. He watched her and there was a sudden warmth in his eyes and for a moment it seemed he wanted to say something, as if he had guessed what was in her mind. They looked at each other, the air alive with tension and an odd lightness filled her head.

"We'd better go or we'll be late," Sam said, breaking the silence.

The moment was gone.

The party cheered her up some. Maya and Joel were there, as well as several other people she knew, and James, whose consulting job at the Rasheed company had come to an end, and was now taking care of a business venture of his own.

"Good evening," he said with mock formality. "And how is the happy couple?"

Sam's face gave nothing away. "Good evening, James. Still here, I see."

"For a while yet." He gave Kim a wolfish grin, which she pretended not to see. He had not been converted by his baptism in the restaurant, and whenever their paths crossed, he was still playing his games. However, Kim had concluded that all was quite innocent and that James was harmless. Not to her surprise, she had also learned that James wasn't exactly an intimate friend of Sam's; they'd simply known each other forever.

"Keep your hands off my wife, pal," Sam said, his voice deceptively even. Kim wondered why he bothered with this display of possessiveness. Irritated, she slipped away to the sound of James's amused laugh and went in search of Maya.

Ten minutes later she found James next to her, all smiles and charm. He put an arm lightly around her shoulder, leaned close and whispered in her ear, telling her a joke, which held her captivated for a moment, and then she laughed. Well it was a funny joke, what else could she do? And as she laughed, she saw Sam watching the two of them and she realized James had purposely orchestrated the little scene, arm around her, whispering in her ear, making her laugh—orchestrated it to antagonize Sam. She caught James looking at Sam, watching for his reaction.

"Why are you trying to aggravate Sam?" she demanded, shaking off his arm.

"Because aggravating him is so much fun." He grinned at her. "Besides," he said, lowering his voice, "I am quite bewitched by you and ever hopeful you will one day find it in your heart to give me a chance."

She made a face at him. "Oh, please."

She was about to march off when Sam arrived on the scene and put a possessive arm around her.

"Is this man bothering you?" he asked her, glaring fiercely at James, who grinned gleefully.

"Oh, I can handle him," she said brightly. This was ridiculous, grown men playing a stupid game. "I'm going outside for some air," she said and swung away from Sam's arm, but he grasped her hand before she could make her escape. "Not so fast, sweetheart," he said. "I'll come with you." And he marched her off determinedly toward the open door into the garden.

"You can quit the protective husband routine," she said coolly. "I can take care of myself."

"James is a womanizer. I don't want you—"

"Don't you think I know that by now?" She gave a brittle little laugh. "Do you think I'm stupid?"

"I didn't say you were stupid, but I know James."

"You weren't concerned about it before," she reminded him.

"Well, I am now," he said curtly.

"Don't be." It was a dark night with only a sliver of a moon and she couldn't decipher the expression on his face, but then she hardly ever could, light or no light. "I know how to handle men like James. It's men like you, who—" She broke off abruptly, cursing herself for not having stopped in time.

"What about men like me?" he asked right on cue.

She shrugged casually. "I've told you. Men who don't talk, who don't show their feelings, who don't let you know what's on their mind. That's the kind I don't know how to deal with." She swung around. "Excuse me, I need to powder my nose."

Sam watched her go, knowing it was no use to go after her. He was acting like a fool, pretending he still had some hold on her. James was not the problem, and he knew it. He himself was the problem.

He looked up at the dark sky and rubbed his neck.

It had all been too good to be true from the start. She had completely bowled him over and he should never have allowed it to happen. He should have known it could never have lasted; one way or another it would have ended.

He should stop hoping. He should stop aching for her. He should just tell her to go home to New York.

What the hell was he thinking?

Kim stood in front of the linen closet, putting away soft piles of freshly laundered towels and sheets she had bought for the house. The washer and dryer had not yet been delivered and Maya had offered Kim the use of her machines to get the job done.

At times Kim wondered if there would ever come an end to all the shopping and buying necessary to get the house in operating order. Still, in earlier times, girls would start work on their trousseaus years before they were even engaged, collecting silverware and dishes and linens, and squirreling them away piece by piece in their hope chests, dreaming of the day the perfect lover would come along and claim them and their embroidered pillowcases.

Kim surveyed the neatly folded linens on the shelves. Such pretty colors, she thought, and suddenly her eyes filled with tears and the colors blurred in front of her.

A flood of emotions overwhelmed her, catching her off guard. She sat down on the floor and let the tears come, unable to stop herself. It was costing her more energy and strength than she could have anticipated to keep up her cool front, to be light and cheerful, to repress her true feelings. It wasn't what she was used to. She didn't know how to be this way. She hated it.

A hand on her shoulder nearly made her jump out of her skin.

It was Nick, looking worried. "Kim? What's wrong?"

She swallowed and tried to compose herself. "I was feeling sorry for myself, that's all." Her voice shook.

"Why?"

"Oh, no reason, really." She scrambled to her feet and grabbed a new box of tissues from one of the shelves. "I have these bouts of sentimentality, they just come over me at the oddest times for no particular reason. It's very inconvenient sometimes, but so far there's no vaccine."

He wasn't amused. "Forgive me for asking, but something is wrong between you and your husband, isn't it?"

She wished she could just tell him about her and Sam, about the ridiculous fake marriage, about the fact that she should never have fallen in love with him, that she had known all along he was the wrong man for her. He didn't talk, he excluded her. He crawled in some dark cave where she wasn't allowed entrance.

She fished out some tissues and mopped her eyes. She'd been stupid. It was her own fault she was in this mess. If she'd just come here to do a job, she'd have been fine, but no, she'd fallen in love with this self-contained, solitary man and now he'd withdrawn for a reason she didn't even know.

She shrugged lightly. "It's nothing," she lied, faking a cheery smile. He just doesn't want me anymore, she added silently, and the thought brought treacherous tears to her eyes again. She turned away quickly, but not fast enough.

Nick's arms came around her and the sudden comfort of his embrace broke all her resistance. Misery poured out of her and to her utter embarrassment she began to sob uncontrollably.

CHAPTER EIGHT

"I'M SORRY," she wept, "I'm sorry."

"It's all right, Kim," Nick said, stroking her hair. "Go ahead and cry, it's all right."

So she cried. There was nothing she could do to stop it, so she just gave into it. After a while she had no more tears.

"What does he do to you?" he asked, his arms still around her. His voice was rough with anger.

"Do to me?" She reached for the tissues. Horror struck her. "No, no!" she said fervently, shaking her head. "He doesn't abuse me if that's what you're thinking."

He scrutinized her silently. "Okay, sorry," he said then.

She wiped her eyes and blew her nose. "We don't...we don't always get along very well," she said lamely. "And, you know, I get tearful over nothing."

Another silence. "Kim," he said then, "will you promise me something?"

"I don't know," she said thickly. "I mean, I don't know if I can."

"If you need help, anything at all, will you let me know?"

His kindness nearly made her start crying again. She nodded. "Yes, I will." She bit her trembling lip. "Excuse me," she muttered, and dashed into the bathroom. She splashed her face with water, sucked in a few deep breaths and ventured back to Nick, who was still standing near the linen closet.

She managed a tremulous smile. "I thought men were

terrified of weeping women,'' she said, searching for a light touch. To her relief, he grinned.

''Oh, I have a lot of experience. I had a girlfriend once who cried all the time, over everything—a full moon, a squashed frog on the road. I became an expert at giving succor and comfort.''

His tone made her laugh. ''What happened to her?''

''She left me for someone who was even more expert than I. And he had a fancy yacht.''

''You don't seem grief stricken.''

''I can barely remember her name.'' He took her hand. ''Come with me. My mother asked me to get you to try out something she's been concocting in the kitchen. Knowing her cooking, I offer no guarantees as to its edibility.''

Kim chuckled and allowed herself to be maneuvered out of the house and away from her mournful musings.

''Kim?'' asked the voice on the phone. ''This is Joanna.''

Kim was sitting on the edge of her bed and had just finished painting her toenails a deep, shiny coral. ''Oh, hi, Joanna,'' Kim returned. ''How are you?'' Clutching the receiver between her chin and shoulder, she screwed the cap back on the bottle of nail polish.

''I'm fine, thanks. Getting organized for the weekend. I'm calling to ask if you'd drive up to Sarangan with me a little earlier in the afternoon on Saturday. It looks like the men are going to be late and I need to be up there to supervise the dinner preparations.''

Kim felt her heart sinking like a stone. Sarangan. She had completely forgotten about the weekend trip to the mountains, and the thought of spending a whole weekend in close contact with Sam filled her with trepidation.

''I'd love the company,'' Joanna went on, ''and to tell you the truth I'd prefer not sit in the car with these men because all they talk about is business and we won't be able to get a word in crosswise."

Kim stared at her newly polished toenails. The weekend was three days away. How could she have forgotten? How could she get out of it? Her mind was scrambling, but in the second she had before she had to respond to Joanna she didn't manage to come up with any brilliant ideas. She was supposed to be Sam's wife. Joanna's husband was a hotshot of some sort, someone important to the Rasheed company, she wasn't sure to what extent. She felt a sinking sense of inevitability.

"I'd love to ride up with you," she heard herself say.

"I'm really very busy," she said to Sam when he returned from the office an hour later. "I don't feel like going to Sarangan. I'd rather keep working on the house. Can't we get out of it?"

"No, we can't," he said brusquely, loosening his tie, then went on to explain something about not offending their host, who was a major investor and one with much political clout, and the fact that there was important business to discuss. She'd known all that already.

"You go," she said. "I intend to be sick. Dengue fever, malaria, dysentery, take your pick. Make something up. Tell them I'm sorry."

He frowned at her. "It won't work, Kim," he said impatiently. "It's three days away and I understand you already accepted Joanna's offer to drive up with her."

Well, so she had. News traveled fast.

Sam frowned at her. "Besides, you're working too hard as it is and you deserve a break. It's cool and beautiful in the mountains, and you like Joanna. Just enjoy it."

Her problem wasn't the mountains or Joanna; her problem was Sam, spending time with Sam, playing the happy wife. They'd be given a room to share, no doubt.

If only Joanna was Maya, if only she knew Joanna better. She just might confide the truth in her. But Joanna and her husband lived in Jakarta and she'd only met her twice before. Joanna was nice enough, if a bit stuffy for Kim's taste and she just wasn't quite bosom buddy material, the type of person in whom you confided your intimate secrets—like not being married to the man everybody thought was your husband and not wanting to share a bed with him.

Well, Kim thought desperately, maybe spending several hours in the car with Joanna would make her feel comfortable enough to broach the subject of separate bedrooms. She could say Sam snored and kept her awake or something like that. She didn't have to tell her the truth. Surely something could be figured out. It might turn out that Joanna wasn't quite as stuffy as she seemed.

And Sam was right, she needed a break from the blasted house, and living in a hotel was getting on her nerves. So, really, why should she deny herself, after all? She could play being the wife some more, she was really getting good at it anyway. Come to think of it, she deserved an Oscar.

"All right," she said to Sam, "but when I am done with this job for you I expect the best letter of reference you've ever written."

His mouth twitched at the corners, and she wondered if she saw a glimmer of relief in his eyes. "Of course," he said with a formal little incline of his head.

"And a bonus would be nice, too," she added for good measure.

The Suhartono villa lay nestled in a lush garden ablaze with flowers and blooming shrubbery. It had been built during colonial times by the Dutch, and it was owned by her in-laws, Joanna told Kim. It was used by the

extended family for rest and relaxation, to get away from
the tropical heat and the rat race of the capital.

The ride into the mountains had been pleasant enough,
the scenery spectacular, but the conversation not terribly
inspiring. Having grown up the daughter of an American
ambassador, Joanna was much concerned with things
proper and appropriate. All Kim's hopes of confiding her
very inappropriate situation to her had evaporated in the
air-conditioned car.

Joanna showed her around the house, apologizing for
the old-fashioned furnishings, making sure Kim knew
none of it was to her taste. It did not require advanced
mathematics to conclude that with the other guests due
to arrive later, all bedrooms would be in use.

A servant had already taken Kim's luggage to the
room allocated to her and Sam. Joanna left her to freshen
up and then join her for afternoon tea on the veranda.

Kim surveyed the small room. There was one old-
fashioned double bed, a couple of small rattan chairs and
a low table. It was all bright and cozy looking. Much
too cozy. They'd have to share the bed, there was no
other place, no sofa, no big chairs to push together.

With an irritated sigh, Kim told herself to stop ob-
sessing like a Victorian virgin, and began unpacking her
bag.

"May I assume you didn't fess up our farce of a marriage to Mr. Suhartono and ask for another bed or a sofa
somewhere else in the house?" Kim asked Sam. She lay
in bed and watched Sam as he stripped off his shirt and
tossed it on one of the small chairs in their bedroom.

"No," he said, "I did not."

Dinner had been very enjoyable and sipping an after-
dinner espresso in front of a real fire had been a treat.
Now everyone had retired to their various sleeping
places and here they were, she and Sam, alone in their
room. Having excused herself a little before Sam had,

she'd had the chance to get herself ready and get into bed before he'd come into the room.

"So where are you going to sleep?" she asked.

He arched his brows at her. "In the bed," he said bluntly. "It's too damned cold to sleep on the floor and there isn't enough bedding anyway." He disappeared into the bathroom.

Kim had not really expected a different response, but hope sprang eternal. She turned off her bedside lamp, huddled under the covers and closed her eyes, pretending to be asleep when Sam came back into the room a while later. He got into the bed and she felt the mattress sagging under his weight. A click and she knew he'd turned off his light.

"Good night, Kim." He knew she wasn't asleep, of course.

"Good night," she muttered in response.

She lay with her back turned to him, rigid and miserable, wondering how she could possibly sleep with him so close by, hearing his breathing, practically feeling his body warmth. Pretending they were nothing but strangers sharing a bed.

Out of nowhere came a memory, a scene from an old, old movie—she couldn't remember the name. An unmarried, quarreling couple were forced to share a bed in a hotel room and rigged up, somehow, a sheet as a divider across the length of the bed. They had lain on either side of it on the bed, fully clothed, staring up at the ceiling, secretly lusting for each other. She'd been very young and thought it excruciatingly romantic. In spite of herself, Kim smiled. In the movies it was funny and romantic. It was more difficult to find humor and romance in her own real-life situation. It wasn't funny to know that the man lying next to her had once made wonderful love to her and now, for some reason she couldn't begin to understand, was no longer interested.

She adjusted the pillow and pulled the blankets up a little higher. She should try to think of something else, something more cheerful.

Something like what?

Her birthday. Her twenty-seventh, coming up soon. She should have a party, as she had every year. She didn't feel at all inspired to think about planning one. It required festive feelings, which were in short supply at the moment.

She was acutely aware of Sam lying next to her, but tried valiantly to ignore it. The house was very quiet. She listened to the silence, wondering how silence could sound so loud.

She couldn't sleep. She counted backward from a hundred, first in English, then in Indonesian and she was still awake. And inches away was Sam. All she had to do was reach out and touch him, feel his warm skin. For a moment of madness she wished she could simply forget what had happened and snuggle up close to him, kiss him, touch him, make love with him.

She moaned softly into the pillow, overwhelmed by an aching need. Oh, God, she couldn't stand it. She couldn't stand it.

Holding her breath, she slipped out of the softly creaking bed and pulled on her robe over her nightgown. She fumbled around finding the paperback she'd been reading and carefully turned the door handle. Amazingly enough, it made only the faintest of noises and she escaped from the room almost soundlessly.

The fire in the living room was still glowing and she sat down in a deep, upholstered chair close to it and tried to read, but the fire was not bright enough to give her much warmth. Shivering, she glanced around, but found no throw rug or blanket of any sort to keep her warm. This was the tropics—how could it be this cold? She huddled deeper into the chair, pulling her feet underneath her and put a small cushion on her lap for warmth.

She must have dozed off in spite of the chill, because the next thing she was conscious of was being lifted up and carried away. Strong arms around her. Her face against something solid and warm. A chest. She opened her eyes and found herself looking up at Sam's face. She felt the comforting warmth of his body as he held her close against him. She shivered. She was freezing. She couldn't think, only feel. And the feeling was good, warm, blissful.

"What did you think you were doing?" he asked angrily.

"I was reading," she muttered. "I couldn't sleep."

He put her under the covers on his side of the bed, still warm from his body. Oh, bliss. She snuggled deep under the blankets and Sam got in beside her.

"Now, go to sleep," he ordered, as if an order was all it would take to send her off into oblivion.

Her feet felt like blocks of ice. She wanted socks. She had a pair tucked in her running shoes, ready for their planned mountain hike in the morning. She sat up.

"What are you doing now?" he said impatiently.

"I'm just getting my socks. My feet are frozen."

"I'll get them. Where are they?"

She told him and he got up and handed them to her before getting back in bed. Under the blankets, she wrestled the socks on her feet, her fingers stiff with cold. Then she lay back and tried to relax and a wild, uncontrollable shiver ran all through her body.

"Oh, for God's sake, Kim," Sam muttered gruffly. "Come here." He hauled her to him, wrapped himself around her before she could make an objection.

She lay perfectly still, her heart pounding so hard she wondered if he could feel it. His warmth was like a balm soaking into her. She smelled the familiar scent of him, all male and sexy, and it went straight to her head. A wave of longing washed over her, followed by a wave of panic. She couldn't let this happen.

"This is not a good idea, Sam," she muttered into his chest, making a feeble effort to pull away.

"It's the best I could come up with." His arms tightened around her. "It's all right. Just go to sleep." His voice was businesslike.

It was all right, he said. Well, of course. He wasn't a stranger. He was Sam; he knew her well. He was her brother's friend. It was all right for him to hold her and make her warm. This was too ridiculous for words. Why was she thinking these thoughts? As if she had to justify herself to anybody.

With the worst of her chill gone, she was beginning to feel drowsy. Sleep. It would be so good to sleep. Sleep in Sam's arms.

Again, out of nowhere a memory floated into her mind.

Samiir.

Someone, she didn't remember who, but it had not been Sam himself, once told her the meaning of that name. Samiir in Arabic meant he who keeps you company at night.

She smiled against the warm, solid wall of his chest and gave a languorous sigh.

Sam was keeping her company at night.

She felt herself sinking, drifting.

She had a wonderful, sensuous dream about floating, about feeling euphoric, about being surrounded by warmth and love. She was in a magical place, a place out of time and full of enchantment.

All was sweetness and joy and her body felt exquisite—beautiful and sensual and full of trembling desire.

Someone was stroking her with silken touches and she

moaned softly, knowing it was Sam. Sam who loved her. Sam who wanted her.

His hands…so wonderful, so knowing. She sighed blissfully and moved closer against him, closer, closer, searching for his mouth. He kissed her with such tenderness her heart flowed over with love and longing, a glowing that warmed her blood. She kissed him back, her body singing with the rapture of it.

They pleasured each other with soft caresses and secret whispers, with loving hands and hungry mouths. Sweet and slow. There was no hurry.

Sweet and slow.

And easy, so easy. As if it were an intimate, erotic dance they'd danced together a hundred times, floating in each other's arms, soaring together, their movements in perfect harmony.

She drifted into sleep, warm and safe.

Birdsong teased the edges of her consciousness. Sunlight filtered dimly through her closed eyelids. For a while she dozed while images of lovemaking floated through her mind: his hands touching her, his mouth kissing her, the feel of him inside her. A dream of magic and illusion.

She sighed and stirred lazily in the bed, her body heavy.

Arms around her. The warmth of another body next to her. She peered through her lashes. Sam's face. Close. So close.

He was looking at her. Sunlight spilled across the bed, across his bare shoulder and chest. Her heart began to dance.

It had not been a dream.

Yet there had been an unreal quality about it all, as if it had happened out of time, as if somehow it belonged to another reality. Beautiful, mysterious.

His face was dark and unreadable with the sunlight bright behind him. She closed her eyes against the glare.

He put his hand against her cheek. "Kim," he whispered, "I know this—"

Opening her eyes she put her hand over his mouth. "Don't," she whispered. "Please don't, Sam."

Don't say you're sorry. Don't say it shouldn't have happened. Don't spoil the magic.

"Kim..."

"I want to sleep," she murmured, closing her eyes again and burrowing deeper under the covers. Sam's body moved away from her, out of the bed. She heard the bathroom door open and close, felt herself dozing off.

When she awoke again the house was full of noise. The sound of feet walking across creaky wooden floors. People laughing. The smell of coffee teased her nose.

It was time to get up and get ready for their early-morning hike in the mountains. Kim threw the covers off and gasped in the chilly air.

They spent the day in the company of other people, hiking, exploring the town, talking and eating together.

She wondered what Sam was thinking, wondered if he wished it had never happened and simply wanted to forget it. She wished she could read his face, but there was nothing in his expression to tell her anything.

Somewhere deep inside her she felt a flicker of hope. Perhaps not all was lost. Perhaps Sam, somewhere behind all that distance and silence, loved her still. Perhaps in the intimacy of the bed, he'd come out of hiding and loved her.

He said nothing the next day, or the next, yet the knowledge of that enchanted night in the mountains remained in the air between them, faint undercurrents of secret memory.

*   *   *

"I'll only be a minute," Kim said to Tuki as she got out of the car in front of the hotel. She'd been running around town all morning doing a hundred things and she was hot, thirsty and her feet hurt; she'd neglected to put on shoes actually meant to be walked in. And she'd forgotten to bring her notebook, which contained all her lists and phone numbers. It was not one of her more organized mornings, but for once she might be forgiven. She'd been a paragon of organization and efficiency, even if she did say so herself.

In the suite, she kicked off her flimsy sandals and put on light white sneakers. Not a fashion statement, but they felt good on her feet. She gulped down a glass of water, grabbed her notebook and rushed out of the room and along the gallery, watching people eating their lunch in the courtyard restaurant. Instantly her stomach began to squirm with hunger. No time now; she had food in the fridge at the house so she'd have something to eat there. The house was almost ready for occupation. It was a good feeling. Clutching the notebook against her chest, she smiled.

The smile froze on her face. Her feet stopped moving.

Sam was sitting at a table eating lunch. With him was a woman, a very beautiful woman in a cool white dress.

Kim had noticed her before, in the hotel lobby, a guest, she'd assumed. Noticing the woman was unavoidable. Apart from being tall and beautiful, she stood out with her flaming red hair.

Rooted to the spot, Kim watched the two eating their food, talking, which they did with intent attention to each other. Standing there hidden behind a colossal potted palm, Kim felt like a spy in a cheap movie. Why was she doing this? Maybe the redhead was another business consultant, like James, or someone else connected with the new company—an electronics expert, a manager. Why was she standing here like a suspicious housewife spying on her husband who was doing nothing more than having an innocent lunch with an innocent business partner?

The red-haired woman reached out and covered Sam's hand, which rested on the table, a gesture of intimacy not customary between mere business partners or consultants, at least not in Kim's world.

Kim's heart made a sickening lurch.

She watched Sam smile at the woman, a very nice smile, as he grasped her hand and squeezed it in response.

Kim whirled around and rushed away from the scene, her legs trembling, her heart racing. She sagged down on a bench somewhere in the lush tropical garden surrounding the hotel and sucked in deep gulps of hot, humid air. She needed to calm herself before getting back in the car, not wanting Tuki to see her in this agitated state.

She wiped the damp hair out of her face, feeling her cotton dress stick to her body. It was so hot. The woman had looked all cool and elegant in her white dress. Some people always looked cool and elegant, no matter what the weather, but not she. She looked like a dirty dishcloth, she was sure. She felt tears collect in her eyes.

She was so pathetic, she should be ashamed of herself, acting as if she were the frumpy wife dumped for a gorgeous femme fatale.

She wasn't Sam's wife. She didn't even want to be his wife. The redhead could have him. She was welcome to him.

CHAPTER NINE

"KIM? Are you there?" It was Nick's voice calling out from the veranda.

"Yes, come on in." Kim had just finished a solitary dinner of chicken sate, having bought the skewers of spicy meat from the vendor at the corner of the street. She was relieved to have some company and distraction. It had been an endless, miserable afternoon and now it was dark and she didn't want to go back to the hotel to have dinner and run into Sam and maybe the redhead. She simply couldn't cope with it right now.

Nick came into the room, carrying a bottle of wine, which he put on the coffee table. "You're not usually here this late," he said evenly, "but I saw the light, so I thought I'd check to see."

"I had a lot to do," she said, amazed that she managed to sound so casual. She waved at a chair and Nick sat down.

"How are you?" he asked, giving her a searching look.

"Fine," she said automatically, faking a cheerful smile.

"You don't look so fine to me." Apparently she had not deceived him.

The image of Sam holding hands with the redhead had haunted her all afternoon as she worked around the house. Was this woman the so-called problem Sam was dealing with? Was he spending his evenings with her? Was she a former lover, an ex-wife, a new woman in his life? Sam had made love to her, Kim, two nights before. Had it meant nothing? Had it just happened for the simple reason that she'd been handy, in his bed at the time?

Nick's blue eyes looked into hers, holding her gaze. "I saw you at the hotel this afternoon," he said softly.

Which meant he had seen Sam and the woman in white.

She said nothing. She didn't know what to say.

"That louse of a husband of yours is having an affair, isn't he?" His tone had a lethal edge to it and his normally friendly face was hard and angry.

She swallowed painfully. "It looks like it, I suppose." What else could she say? No, I don't think so, there's probably a good explanation why he's holding hands with another woman? Kim shifted restlessly in her chair and tucked her feet underneath her.

"Do you know her?"

She shook her head. "No. I've seen her around the hotel a couple of times." She didn't want to talk about it. Sam romancing another woman was not an uplifting subject of conversation.

Nick came to his feet and jammed his hands into his pockets. "You were married a couple of months ago, just before you came here, isn't that what you told my mother? Why did you marry him, Kim?"

She gave a tortured little laugh. I didn't marry him, she wanted to say, but she couldn't bring herself to tell him the truth. It was too embarrassing for words. "I was stupid, I guess," she said, staring down at her hands in her lap, not wanting to look at him. "I don't really want to talk about it right now."

"I'm not trying to pry, Kim, but I care about you and I worry."

"I know," she said quietly. He was trying to be a friend. He was being a friend.

"When I first met you, you were happy and vivacious

and you had lights in your eyes. And now…'' He shook his head. "I don't like what I see."

She managed a smile. "Just a temporary dimming of the lights. Don't worry, I'll be fine." She gestured at the bottle of wine he'd put on the table.

"What's that for?"

"I just got a contract to do another series of articles and wanted to celebrate."

"Oh, Nick, that's great! Congratulations!" She leaped to her feet. "I'll get a corkscrew and some glasses."

"I brought a corkscrew, just in case," he said, fishing it out of the pocket of his khaki shorts.

After he had left, an hour later, Kim wondered why she couldn't just stay right here for the night instead of going back to the hotel and maybe running into Sam. The bathroom had already been stocked with toiletries. There was fruit and cheese in the kitchen. She'd given the new washer and dryer a test run and had clean clothes to wear. She couldn't think of a good reason, so she made up the bed in one of the guest rooms.

She was tired but restless and she knew she wouldn't sleep. She might as well do something useful. In the living room she began to pry the newly purchased TV set, VCR and CD player out of their cardboard boxes.

Plugging in the television and making it work was easy. She even found an English-language movie on one of the channels, an old one, a love story. Leaving it turned on she began setting up the CD player.

She was sitting cross-legged on the Chinese rug, reading the installation instructions, when she heard Sam's voice calling out to her from the entry hall. Her heart lurched. It was late. What was he doing here?

"Why are you still here?" he asked, coming into the living room. Deep lines of fatigue sharpened his features. Exhausted from entertaining the redhead, no doubt, she thought, feeling herself grow cold.

"I'm working," she said coolly. "And why are you here?"

He studied her for a moment. "I was worried about you."

"Worried?" She almost laughed. "Why?"

"You're always home when I get there, Kim. You weren't tonight."

She shrugged. "There's a lot to do, I got busy." Her tone was curt and she didn't look at him as she spoke.

"Is something wrong?"

She had her lead. She could tell him that indeed something was wrong, that she had seen him holding hands with that woman, that she was tired of playing games, that she thought he was a miserable excuse of a man.

She didn't have the energy.

What good would it do? The solution to her miseries was simple: Go back to New York and forget Sam.

"I have a headache," she said. It was true enough—if not a physical headache at least a mental and emotional one. A migraine, really. She untangled her legs and scrambled up from the carpet, wincing at the prickly pain in her feet; they were asleep.

Sam frowned at her. "You'd better stop now and come back to the hotel with me. Take some aspirin and go to bed. By the way, where's Tuki?"

"I sent him home. I'm going to stay here tonight."

His frown deepened. "Why?"

"That way I can get started right away in the morning." It was true enough.

"There's no need for you to work day and night, besides, I don't want you staying here all by yourself in this empty house."

"I'll be fine," she said coolly.

A silence ensued and she noticed Sam's gaze settling on the bottle of Chardonnay and the two glasses on the coffee table. "Then again," he said slowly, meaningfully, "maybe you won't be by yourself."

Hot anger rushed through her. How dare he suggest this? He, who was having a fling with that woman in her cool white dress. She was tempted to scream at him, but refused to turn into a jealous, yelling wife.

She didn't want him to know how miserable he made her. It was so humiliating. And then another emotion took over. Exhaustion. *I don't care anymore,* she thought, weariness overwhelming her. It was all a hopeless mistake and she had brought it on herself. She would just have to get over it. She hugged herself and turned toward the window, not responding to his insinuation.

"Is Nick staying here with you tonight?" he demanded, his face like stone.

She wasn't sure what happened in her head, what crazy button was pushed. She swung around and gave him a taunting smile.

"Yes," she said, "and a few other men are coming as well. I'm planning an orgy—drinking, dancing, debauchery and lots of sex the whole night through."

"You're being vulgar," he said with distaste.

She gave him a cheery smile. "But I'm having so much fun! You could join us, if you like, bring your girlfriend. She looks like she could use some loosening up."

He stared at her with narrowed eyes. "What's gotten into you?" he asked sharply.

She shrugged carelessly. "I have no idea what you mean. I like parties, I like a bit of fun and cheer, you know that."

He turned away, then stopped and regarded her with a quizzical look on his face.

"What girlfriend?"

"You have more than one? I was thinking of the redhead you had lunch with today. She was holding your hand and looking adoringly at you with those big brown puppy eyes."

"Lunch? Oh, yes, I see." He smiled wryly. "I assure you, she's not the object of my amorous affections."

"Maybe she's your loving sister, Yasmina, coming to your aid in a time of stress?" She didn't like the sarcastic note in her voice, but it just sort of popped right in there. If he were going through a difficult time, it wasn't funny, but he certainly had not sought solace from her, the woman he'd been sleeping with at the time the crisis had struck.

He smiled faintly. "A sister, Yasmina, really would come in handy, wouldn't it? No, the lady in question is Katherine Dumas, and she's one of our company lawyers, as well as an old family friend. She's here in an official capacity, dealing with legal matters."

"I see," she said, not sure what to think. "And holding hands with her is part of dealing with legal matters, I suppose?" She shouldn't have said that, she knew the moment the words were out. She sounded suspicious, jealous, bitchy—all the things she didn't want to be, all the things she didn't want him to notice.

There was a dark shimmer in his eyes, amusement? She wasn't sure. His mouth curved up at one corner. "No, that was the old friend coming through."

How touching, she almost said, swallowing the words just in time. He could be lying through his teeth, how would she know? Then again he could be telling the truth. All she had seen was the woman putting her hand on Sam's, which could be nothing more than a simple gesture of comfort or encouragement from a person he knew well. Kim shrugged indifferently. "Oh, well, my mistake."

On the TV screen the two lovers were talking. The woman was crying. The hero took her in his arms and

kissed her. Kim glanced away from the screen. She felt
in serious need of some good old-fashioned crying, in
need of some good old-fashioned comfort from a loving,
understanding man. She wasn't going to get it. She
wanted Sam out of the house. She wanted to be alone.

She ran her fingers through her hair and met his gaze
straight on. "I know this is your house, but I would
appreciate it if you would leave now," she said with a
calmness she didn't know she possessed. "It's late and
I'm tired."

Without another word in response, Sam strode to the
door, then turned abruptly to face her. "I have to go
back to New York again. I'm leaving in the morning.
I'll be gone about a week."

A message from Jason! Kim was calling up her e-mail
messages on the computer in the hotel room, as she did
every morning as soon as she got up. She loved the stuff
her friends sent her and they'd faithfully kept in touch
with her. Even Jason had written a couple of times, saying he missed her, and that the friend to whom she had
sublet the loft was bossy and disturbed his peaceful hermit existence. Come back soon! he ended his missives.

As Kim read his latest message, her heart began to
pound and she forgot to breathe. "I read it in the paper,"
Jason had written, "but I imagine you already know."

No, she hadn't known.

Sam had been gone two days. She'd done little but
work. She was sleeping at the hotel, but was hardly ever
there and hadn't read the American papers that were
delivered to their suite every day.

"Oh, no," she whispered. "Oh, no." She read and
reread the message, numb with shock.

Sam was being sued. Sued by a woman who claimed
he was the father of her unborn baby.

CHAPTER TEN

For days Kim's mind was in turmoil as she tried to make sense of the sordid story. Why had Sam not told her? Because it was true and he didn't know how to tell her? Instead of telling her he had retreated from her, crawled into some cold, lonely hole where she couldn't reach him. She could only imagine what the humiliation was doing to a man like Sam.

Could the story really be true? The shoddy tale she read in the paper seemed damning enough. Cheap and damning. The woman in question wasn't anyone he'd known, just a woman who had stayed the night at his Santiago apartment once, with witnesses to prove it. Kim had trouble reading all the sordid details and tossed the paper away in disgust. She wanted to hear the story from Sam, not read this sensationalistic stuff in the papers.

It was difficult seeing the Sam she knew as the man portrayed in the story, a wealthy, ruthless businessman, an electronics baron, they called him, taking advantage of a naive little secretary whom he'd lured into bed after a party at his house after first tempting her to drink several strong drinks. Only the naive secretary was twenty-four years old. How naive could you be at twenty-four?

Well, Kim thought, *I'm almost twenty-seven and how naive am I?* It was a disturbing thought.

Damn Sam, damn him for not telling her.

Nick had taken it upon himself to cheer her up and give her some diversion. Kim accepted with both hands. She had a life to live and Nick was great company.

One day they went to see the huge Borobudur temple,

an ancient Buddhist shrine, one of the ten wonders of
the world, and climbed all the hundreds of steps to the
top. Nick had taken pictures of her, as he was taking
pictures of her all the time.

They were both exhausted when they got back to the
hotel and crashed on the sofa, too weary to move a limb.
When hunger struck Nick ordered some food from room
service for which he paid with cash, not allowing her to
pay her share or put it on the bill.

The food finished, Nick climbed reluctantly to his feet.
"I'd better be going." He smiled down at her, his blue
eyes warm. "I had a terrific day, Kim. I'm glad you
could come with me."

"Me, too," she said, and stifled a yawn. She laughed.
"Sorry."

"Go to bed," he ordered. "I'll talk to you tomorrow." He stalked toward the door.

The door opened before Nick got to it, and Sam strode
in, tall, imposing, filling the doorway. Sam, wearing
jeans, a polo shirt, carrying a briefcase and a laptop computer, obviously just off a plane.

Sam, back from New York, looking devastatingly
handsome.

In spite of everything, the feminine part of her reacted
to him, standing there radiating an unmistakable masculine appeal. Her heart beat erratically and for a moment her breath stuck in her throat. All her senses clam-
oring, she was no longer tired. For that one moment she
only saw him, every facet of his face, his dark, compelling eyes, the square shape of his shoulders, the casual
look of him in well-fitting jeans. For that one fleeting
moment she felt awash with warmth and emotion and
treacherous yearning for love, for understanding, for a
miracle.

Sam stopped in the doorway, looked at Nick and then

at Kim, his face freezing into stone, his eyes black and cold.

Kim no longer felt warm.

"Good evening," said Nick politely.

Sam glared at him, his jaw rigid. "What the hell are you doing here?" he demanded harshly.

"Keeping your wife company." Nick's face gave nothing away. His voice was perfectly neutral, as if he'd merely announced to have fixed a plumbing problem.

"Get out of my room," Sam said, enunciating each word, dark menace in his voice.

Nick inclined his head slightly. "I was just leaving," he said calmly, as if not at all perturbed by Sam's hostility. "Good night, Kim." He strode through the open door and Sam, with utmost restraint, closed it quietly behind him. Sam did not slam doors.

Kim had come to her feet and put the empty coffee cups on the room service table. She had to do something, anything to get her anger under control. Her hands were shaking. She resented the fact that Sam somehow had the power to make her feel defensive, almost guilty, as if he'd found them in a state of undress, doing sexual acrobatics on the sofa. It was ridiculous. There was nothing to be guilty about. Not even, she reminded herself, if he had found them naked on the sofa.

"You have no right to treat my friends in that hostile manner," she said, trying to sound calm, but hearing the unmistakable tremor of fury in her voice. "It's uncalled for and inappropriate."

"It is inappropriate for you to be entertaining a man in this suite when I am not present."

She laughed, she couldn't help it. She sagged weakly back onto the sofa.

"You find this amusing?" he asked imperiously.

"Oh, come off it! You sound like somebody out of a Victorian novel! May I remind you that the two of us sharing this suite is probably even more inappropriate? Speaking in Victorian terms of course.''

"I don't want that man in this room," he snarled. "Is that phrased more to your liking?"

"No," she snapped back, "it is not. I live here. Where else would I invite my friends to come?"

His eyes narrowed, his jaw grew steely. "He is not your friend. How stupid do you think I am? The man is besotted with you. If you want to conduct an affair with him, do it somewhere else."

He strode into his bedroom before she was able to say a word in return. She stared at the door closing behind him, trembling with rage, her hands balled into fists by her side.

"I hate you," she whispered at the door, hot tears filling her eyes. Then, on impulse, she marched right up to the door and flung it open, blinking furiously to clear her vision. He was searching for something in the open briefcase on his bed and glanced up, brows arched at her unexpected intrusion.

"Listen," she said sharply, her hands on her hips for good measure, her feet anchored to the floor, "I know you're in deep trouble and that you've just spent God knows how long on a wretched plane, but don't you dare take your miseries out on me or my friends!" She spun around and, feeling no qualms about slamming doors, she slammed the door shut behind her.

She felt better. Much better.

It was not a feeling that lasted.

She thrashed around in bed for hours, half-asleep, half-awake, her mind going around in circles. She kept looking at the bedside clock in despair: 1:12, 2:10, 2:40.

Through the closed door noises drifted in from the sitting room. She lay still and listened. Sam, prowling around. Sam, awake.

She staggered out of bed, wrestled her arms through

the sleeves of her kimono and opened her bedroom door, not knowing what drove her. Something…this aching need to talk to Sam, to know the truth, to know what was going on in his head, to understand him.

You're crazy, a little voice inside her said. He's not like you. He doesn't want to lay bare his soul. Why do you even try? It won't lead to anything. You and Sam, it's a hopeless cause.

Sam stood by the window, wearing nothing but a pair of jeans, his dark hair falling over his forehead. He needed a haircut, she thought irrelevantly. Although, come to think of it, it looked rather sexy, this slightly unkempt look of him with his bare feet and bare brown torso. More approachable, somehow.

He turned his face and met her eyes. He just stood there, not saying a word, just looking. Something in his eyes made her turn weak in the knees, made her heart ache for him. He had the haunted look of someone trapped behind bars.

"Couldn't sleep?" she inquired unnecessarily.

"No." He raked his hand through his unruly hair, not taking his gaze away from her face. "I want to apologize for letting off steam at you and…Nick." He sounded calm. "You were quite right, it was uncalled for."

"It's all right," she said, feeling magnanimous.

His eyes were smoky and unreadable. "I wasn't expecting to find him here."

"We'd been out all day, doing tourist stuff. We went to the Borobudur temple and climbed all the way to the top. We got back late and we were exhausted, so instead of going out again to eat we ordered room service. He was just about to leave when you came home."

"You don't owe me an explanation, you know."

"I know." She took in a fortifying breath and made herself look right at him. "Sam, I know why you went to New York," she said carefully.

"Really," he said, without inflection. He shoved his hands into the pockets of his jeans and glanced out the window.

"It's a small world, you know. News travels fast. E-mail, phones, faxes."

"Well," he said flatly, "then I assume you are well-informed."

His tone irked her. Did he think she was gullible? That she'd blindly believe whatever story she heard or read?

"I haven't heard your side," she said curtly. "At least not coming straight from you."

"No, you haven't." His face closed up, his eyes grew distant. He turned his head and stared back out the window.

She began to feel a rising anger. "Why didn't you tell me? A little openness on your part would add immeasurably to your charm."

"It had nothing to do with you," he said harshly, "and I'm used to solving my own problems. There's no point involving you in this unsavory business."

Something snapped in her, she could almost hear it happen in her head. "Will you drop the act!" she burst out. "Will you drop that goddamned gentlemanly reserve and talk to me! Tell me what you feel! How do you expect people to love you and care for you if you don't let them know what goes on inside of you? Tell me what you feel!" She felt like a rudderless boat charging ahead in a turbulent sea. She could crash into the rocky coast of some uninhabited island and smash to pieces. She didn't care. It didn't matter anymore. She had nothing to lose.

He took her by the arm, pushed her down in a chair and stood there looming over her, intimidating her with his sheer size and strength. "Calm yourself down," he ordered, as if she were an unruly child who needed discipline.

She wanted to run, to get away from this man and collapse somewhere in a corner and be alone, but he had her blocked in and she couldn't move. Rigid with anger, she glared up at his implacable face.

"I don't want to calm down! I want you to tell me what you are afraid of!"

His left brow arched imperiously, as if the very thought of his being afraid of anything was ludicrous. He made no reply.

"Are you afraid to talk to me because it's true what they said in the papers?" she taunted. "Because you're humiliated and your precious male ego is smashed to bits and your true odious self has been exposed to the whole world and your reputation is ruined until eternity and you can't face yourself least of all me, and here you are, saddled with a kid you don't want and for whom you'll have to take responsibility for the next eighteen years or so and whose very existence will remind you of your own sorry failings till the day you die and—" She stopped, unable to think of what to say next and to her surprise she saw Sam's face and the faint but unmistakable amusement in his expression.

"Do go on," he invited, his voice dry.

"No," she said, "I'll save my breath." It was hopeless, useless, she might as well give up and save her passions for a more viable cause such as world brotherhood and eternal peace. She pulled her legs up and wrapped her arms around them. She closed her eyes and rested her forehead on her knees. "Go away," she said.

He stepped back from her chair. She heard him move to the other side of the room, heard him pour himself a drink.

"You want a brandy?" he asked, ever the gentleman.

"No, thank you." She'd just about lost her mind; drink was not going to help.

"A drink will do you good."

She raised her head and gave him a withering look. "I'm doing just fine, thank you," she declared, a brave statement in view of all the evidence to the contrary. Whatever it was she might need, it wasn't brandy. She couldn't stand the stuff. She couldn't stand him, looming there in his bare chest with that glass in his hand, all manly control, loftily amused at her ravings. Yet when she looked in his eyes there was something else—dark shadows and the distant flickering of something not at all composed.

Her heart stumbled. No, she was imagining it.

Drawing in a ragged breath, she looked away from his face, her gaze coming to rest on his chest. It was not a good place to linger; it was wide, tanned, covered with a light matt of dark curly hair, and it evoked feelings that were not at all useful right at the moment.

He lowered himself onto the sofa across from her, took a drink from his glass and stared off into space.

"This whole godforsaken lawsuit is a scheme, a setup," he said harshly, his jaw hard. "The woman lied. She made up the whole story and lied."

Kim stared at him, surprised he was talking. "Why?" she asked quietly.

His mouth turned down with unconcealed disgust. "Money, what else," he said contemptuously.

Kim didn't know what to say.

"I had a cocktail party at my house in Santiago one night," he went on, his voice tense. "A lot of people. She was there, but I don't know who'd invited her, because I certainly hadn't. I didn't know her. I'd never seen her before." He closed his eyes and rubbed his neck. "She wasn't well," he said flatly. "She fainted. When she came to, we put her in a guest room and she fell asleep. When everyone was leaving we decided not to wake her. Nobody seemed to know where she lived or who had brought her. It was late and I figured we'd worry about it in the morning.'' He grimaced with self-derision. ''Anyway, I went to bed. Next morning I woke up and went to check on her and heard her in the bathroom, vomiting.''

''She was already pregnant,'' said Kim.

''Yes.''

It didn't take much imagination to see what had happened, what had gone through the woman's mind: she'd seen Sam, she'd seen his house, she'd seen her chance. Or maybe it was all planned beforehand. She'd fabricated her story of seduction and gone to a lawyer.

''My housekeeper was in the kitchen and did not witness this lovely little scene,'' he went on. ''She produced a hearty breakfast, but our pregnant lady only nibbled on some toast and made cheerful conversation, some of which I was not witness to as I went to answer the phone in the living room. Suffice to say that what was said was not in my favor. My housekeeper, who was newly hired, is now a witness for her side.''

He was full of rigidly contained anger, she could tell from the hot flickering in his eyes, the tension in the muscles of his neck and shoulders.

''I'm having to defend myself against despicable charges,'' he said. ''Charges that are false. My integrity is being questioned, my name is being dragged through the gutter.'' He closed his eyes briefly, clenching his jaws, and she saw the effort it took him to speak, recognized the pain hidden beneath the anger.

Her heart softened and she suppressed the urge to go up to him and put her arms around him. She watched him in silence, waiting, hoping he would not close down now and stop talking.

''I do not go around randomly seducing strange women,'' he said roughly, ''I do not go around impregnating women. I do not ever, ever shirk or deny my legitimate responsibilities.''

She thought of his trip to Jordan, of cutting everything short in New York in order to take care in person of the needs of an old grandmother who, blind and almost deaf, no longer even knew who he was; to see to the needs of scores of other relatives, because it was his duty and because he wanted to and they counted on him for more than just his money.

He came to his feet, restless, his body tense. "We haven't even been to court yet and the world has already made up its collective mind about the kind of person I am, and even winning the case is not going to erase all the damage that has been done. It certainly isn't doing the company's reputation any good."

"What are your lawyers saying?" she asked. "Will you win?"

"We think we will. This woman was certainly naive in some matters. There are medical ways to prove this baby isn't mine. The whole situation is outrageous, pathetic, really," he said grimly. He raked his hands through his hair impatiently, as if trying to find some order somewhere, anywhere. "I don't want to go into the sordid details." He came to his feet, stalked to the window and stared into the darkness.

Kim's heart contracted. He looked lost and confused, his shoulders slightly hunched, his hair falling over his forehead. Lost and confused—such a strange sentiment to have about Sam.

"One day it will all be over," she said prophetically, if not profoundly. "And your name will be cleared and you can go on with your life." A little optimism seemed to be in order.

He turned to face her, the right corner of his mouth curving down, doubt in his eyes. "You believe me?"

"Yes."

He stared at her. "Why? What makes you think I'm not just making up my side of the story?"

"Intuition." She gave a half smile. She knew he was telling the truth. She didn't know why she knew, she just did.

He shook his head. "You amaze me," he said. "I'm not sure I would believe me."

"Maybe you're too rational," she said, coming to her feet and standing next to him by the window. "Being rational doesn't always lead us to the truth."

If I were rational, she thought, *I would have left here last month. If I were rational I would never have come here in the first place. If I were rational I would not love this man.*

He closed his eyes for a moment, then reached out and took her hand and squeezed it. He gazed into her eyes, his mouth curved in a hint of a smile.

"Thank you," he said quietly.

The feel of his hand around hers, the softly spoken words opened something inside her, a swell of emotions, an ocean of need to put her arms around him and hold him tight. She stood motionless, terrified she would do something incredibly stupid. His gaze locked with hers, and she felt as if she were drowning.

Time stood still. His face moved toward her as if in slow motion. She closed her eyes, felt his mouth on hers.

"Thank you," he repeated, whispering against her lips.

A heart-stopping moment of promise, of hope.

Then it was over as he drew away abruptly. It was too short a kiss, it left her hungering for more, for everything. She ached with the need to hold him, but he had stepped back outside her reach.

She looked into his eyes, and in the silence she sensed his struggle for control, sensed him pulling back from her, from his own emotion, the outrage he'd vented to her. Perhaps he'd revealed more than he had intended, more than he was comfortable with and he needed distance.

"Two more hours before sunrise," he said evenly, his face revealing no emotion. "We'd better see that we get some more sleep."

She nodded, avoiding his gaze, afraid he'd read in her eyes what she was feeling—her need for him, the longing to be in his arms. She turned and took refuge in her room.

Miracles of miracles, she managed to sleep.

She awoke with a feeling of lightness. She lay still and tried to think why, and it took hardly any time at all. She felt light because the invisible burden of misery had been lifted magically. Sam had come back from New York and he had told her the story. He had actually talked to her, exposing his emotions. His anger was more than just anger, she knew. It covered up the pain and helplessness of having been falsely accused of acts and behavior alien to his character. His integrity, his sense of honor had been violated.

And he had kissed her, which definitely had had a dizzying effect on her, although the kiss had been short and delicate as if he had been afraid to touch her, afraid to get too close.

Well, today was another day, a day with new possibilities. She swung her legs over the edge of the bed and sat for a moment smiling happily at nothing in particular.

She was hopeless, really. Except that she did not at all feel hopeless. She felt quite exuberant, vivacious, alive, ready to dance into a new day.

She needed her head examined. Was she going to allow herself to be swept away once again?

Yes, she was. She loved being swept away, she loved the feeling of it, the joy and expectation and hope and how it made the world seem like such a marvelous place.

Grinning to herself, she lifted her arms above her head, linked her fingers and stretched herself as high as she could.

Noises from the living room. Voices, the faint clink of china, the sound of a door closing. Sam was up and had ordered breakfast. She couldn't remember the last time he'd eaten breakfast in the room. She felt suddenly ravenously hungry and leaped to her feet, pulled on her kimono and went to investigate.

"Good morning," said Sam. He was dressed in a suit and tie, the dynamic businessman again, a man in control of his life. He was reading the *Herald Tribune*, drinking coffee. "Hope I didn't wake you."

She waved her hand. "No, no. Is there coffee for me?" A dumb question. One quick glance at the table told her that there was an abundance of food, juice and coffee. She caught the glint of humor in Sam's eyes.

"I ordered a whole pot, just in case you woke up. I know how much you love your caffeine fix in the morning."

"Oh, thank you. And chocolate croissants, too. Oh goodie." She poured some coffee, took one of the buttery, flaky rolls and settled on the sofa to indulge. "Did you get some sleep?" she asked, having had a good drink from the strong, hot coffee.

"Not much. How about you?"

"I slept a little." She took a bite from the croissant, spreading buttery flakes everywhere. "So, what's new in the paper this morning?" she asked. "Do we have world peace yet?"

"Sorry, no."

She sighed. "I'm beginning to lose my patience, I tell you." She took another bite.

Giving her an amused look, Sam folded the paper and deposited it on the table. "I'd better get started on my working day," he commented, coming to his feet.

"Oh, I didn't tell you yet," said Kim, brushing crumbs from her lap onto a plate, "but if you want to, we can move into the house today. The beds are made and there's food in the fridge."

He looked pleasantly surprised. "Excellent, I'm impressed."

"There are a few more things to be done, mostly in terms of the decorating, but I can do that while we're there."

He nodded. "Good, I'm getting ready to get out of this hotel. What about servants?"

"All taken care off. They came to the house a few days ago so I could show them around and make up a work schedule and so forth, and tomorrow they're starting officially. Give us a couple of weeks and we'll have your household running like a Maserati."

He laughed. "I don't doubt it for a moment."

"And I'll get started on the planning for the party. I assume you'll want a formal sort of affair, something sophisticated with elegant food and...oh, you do still want a party?"

"Of course, but there's no hurry. Let's get settled in first." He put his hand on the doorknob. "Unless you're in a hurry to get back to New York?"

It was said casually enough, yet her silly heart began to flutter nervously. What did he mean by that? Did he mean anything at all? His expression was perfectly neutral.

"No hurry at all," she said, equally casually.

CHAPTER ELEVEN

KIM moved her clothes and other personal belongings to the house that morning. The guest room she had chosen for herself was big and airy and had a view of the walled-in garden. She stood in front of the window for a moment, enjoying the scenery.

The gardener was watering the new lawn. A purple bougainvillea bush splashed its color along the stone wall, and the sun drenched the world in liquid gold. Birds chirped blissfully and Kim found herself humming as she mulled over the possibilities for dinner.

Siti, the cook, had arrived in the morning and Kim had sent her off to the *passar* for fresh produce, shrimp and meat. Rice, pasta and spices already filled the shelves of the pantry and coming up with a nice meal would not be a big challenge.

Sam called early in the afternoon and just hearing his voice over the phone made her heart leap.

"I just want to double-check you're ready to vacate the hotel," he said.

"Absolutely. I am planning dinner, even."

He laughed. "We could eat out, Kim. Make it easy on yourself."

"No, no. It's the first night in your very own home. You should sit at your own dining-room table, eating a home-cooked meal from your own kitchen. I'm going to cook up a storm."

"You did hire a cook, didn't you?" He sounded vaguely worried.

"Siti, yes. We're both going to cook up a storm."

He laughed. "I'd better not be late coming home, then."

"Better not," she agreed, injecting threat in her tone.

Kim spent the next couple of hours in the kitchen with Siti preparing dinner. The dining-room table had been set, flowers had been arranged and candles were ready to be lit.

Beautiful, clean and fragrant, the house was ready for occupation. She had done a superb job and she felt a wonderful sense of satisfaction. Sam, of course, had not been involved in any extensive way and how he would feel about the finished look of the place was still to be seen. He'd been too preoccupied with rescuing his reputation from the viciousness of a greedy woman, she reminded herself. He'd been tormented by malicious publicity. She'd just have to forgive him. She grinned to herself.

"Okay, I forgive you," she said out loud, and felt a little foolish.

Nick dropped by with a collection of photographs, close-ups he had taken of her a few days ago. They were great photos, even Kim had to admit it. Usually she wasn't all that happy with pictures of herself. Nick was a very good photographer, but then, he was a professional.

"You look chipper today," he stated, studying her. "I was a little concerned, actually, after I left last night."

Meaning he was concerned because Sam had been angry, worrying he'd find her here in a sorry state of distress once again. She wasn't distressed. She felt quite undistressed, especially thinking about the way Sam had kissed her last night. This, however, wasn't something she was about to reveal to Nick.

Her gaze fixed on the photographs, she made a dismissive gesture. "Sam apologized for blowing up the way he did. He spent two days on a plane, practically without sleep. He'd been dealing with a crisis in New York and he was exhausted.'' Such a good wife she was, making excuses for her husband. She glanced up at Nick and smiled. ''Thanks so much for these pictures. They're great.''

''You're very welcome.'' He gave a crooked grin. ''I find you a very inspiring subject.''

''Why, thank you, sir,'' she said sweetly. ''I'm flattered. No man has ever called me an inspiring subject.''

She offered him some iced tea, but he declined, saying he had to pack. ''I'll be off tomorrow morning for Surabaya,'' he told her, raising his long body out of the chair. ''I'll be back Monday night.''

Monday was her birthday. She hadn't been in the mood for a party, so she hadn't planned anything to celebrate. It was too late now.

After Nick had left, she went to her room and had a shower, washed her hair, polished her nails and generally primped, dressed and adorned herself until she was satisfied with her appearance. Not too sophisticated and elegant, but still feminine and pretty. A cool, summery dress of white and sky blue, sleeveless and slim, hugged her hips and reached down to her ankles. High-heeled sandals made her look taller. Long dangling earrings shimmered like drops of blue water in the light. She left her hair loose, the curls swept back on one side and tamed by a large comb.

Then she gave herself a talking to. She was going to play it cool. She was not going to do anything stupid, like show him how much she had missed him and wanted him back. She was going to stay poised and calm. There was no need to splash her every emotion into her facial expressions and words.

When she heard him come through the front door, her heart slammed against her ribs and she forgot to breathe. How was she possibly going to keep her face neutral?

"Welcome home," she said, smiling at him much too brightly, she was sure, but she just couldn't help herself. Sam carried an armload of flowers and a bottle of champagne. He looked wonderful and sexy and she couldn't help responding to it.

"Thank you." He smiled. "I brought you flowers, and champagne to celebrate. Something smells wonderful."

"Thank you. The flowers are beautiful. Let's sit on the veranda to have the champagne," she suggested. She took the flowers from him. "I'll put these in a vase and get some glasses."

A few moments later she stepped through the big double doors onto the veranda, finding Sam, hands in his pockets, strolling from one end of the veranda to the other, surveying his surroundings.

The wide veranda was like an outdoor room with rattan furniture with batik fabric cushions, a couple of standing lamps to give light after dark, an overhead fan to stir the air and large potted plants everywhere to create a gardenlike atmosphere. A bamboo wind chime gave soft, haunting sounds, reminders of the tropical forests.

"This is magnificent," he said.

She felt a warm glow of pleasure. "I'm glad you like it." She lowered herself into one of the chairs. "I think the veranda is the best place in the whole house."

"I think you're right." He sat down as well and reached for the bottle of champagne. He popped it open, filled the two glasses and handed her one.

She lifted her glass to his. "Let's have a toast. That you may live here happily, have many friends and good fun and find success in your work."

"Thank you." One corner of his mouth lifted in a half smile. He clinked his glass to hers. "I appreciate all the hard work you've put into this place."

"I enjoyed it." Warm, fuzzy feelings embraced her.

"And now," said Sam, "there's more to celebrate."

"Really? What?" But she knew before he answered, saw the relief of it in his face.

"The lawsuit has been dropped," he said.

Happiness suffused her. "Oh, Sam, this is wonderful! I'm so happy for you!" She wanted to hug him, but they were sitting there with their full glasses in their hands and she'd have to put hers down, get up, move over to his chair, bend over…and then he'd still have his glass in his hands… So she stayed in her chair and kept smiling, lifting her glass once more to make another toast.

Dinner was a success, the food delicious, the conversation easy enough—but then she never had much trouble talking. She was gabbing too much, probably, but Sam didn't seem bored.

She found herself telling him about the parties she liked to give in her loft in New York, and about the time she had almost been arrested, along with a group of her friends.

Her parties always had a theme, a pretext or a reason, she explained. She'd had a party on the Saturday following the first day of spring, as she had every year, and she'd asked everyone to bring wildflower seeds. In the middle of the night they'd all gone out and lavishly sprinkled boxes and boxes of seeds in empty lots, by the roadsides, in any small patch of barren dirt they came across. Their charitable intentions misunderstood, they had almost been arrested by an overzealous policeman.

"Imagine you in a New York City jail," Sam said dryly.

"I'd rather not," she returned and laughed. It probably wasn't the sort of situation in which a real Mrs. Rasheed would be expected to find herself. Then of course, she wasn't a real Mrs. Rasheed.

She put her fork down. "I promise the party I'm or-

ganizing for you will not involve the sprinkling of wildflower seeds or my getting arrested for some transgres-
sion." At least she hoped not.

"What are you planning?" he asked, looking faintly
suspicious. Was he really suspicious, she wondered, or
did he just pretend to be? She probably would have been
wiser not to have told him about her misadventure, but
that was the problem with her, always talking too much.

"I'm planning something very proper and dignified,"
she said reassuringly, trying to look somber and serious.
"I can do that, you know, if I really apply myself."

"Sounds like you're planning a funeral," he said
wryly.

She laughed. "All right, how about if I say I'm planning something sophisticated and upscale in harmony
with your elevated status in the business community?"

He raised one eyebrow and gave her a dubious look.
She sighed heavily. "I know, I know. It will be a challenge for me, not being terribly sophisticated and upscale, myself."

"I know," he commiserated, "you poor hillbilly from
the back of beyond."

She glowered at him. "Go ahead, make fun of me."

"You're asking for it," he said mildly. "I suggest you
don't worry about it. I'm more interested in people having a good time than in making any particular impression."

She grinned. "That will make things a lot less complicated."

So they discussed the party some more while savoring
the luscious dessert of mango mousse she'd made that
afternoon, and that consumed, she suggested they go into
the sitting room for coffee. She excused herself for a
moment to check on the state of affairs in the kitchen.

Having ascertained that the tireless Siti was in full
control of the proceedings, she sashayed into the sitting

room, feeling quite victorious. Everything was going so well. Siti was as good as her previous employers had said. Sam was relaxed and had enjoyed the meal. And best of all, the lawsuit had been dropped and Sam's nightmare was over. It was enough to make her want to do a little waltz around the room.

She found Sam looking at the pictures Nick had brought that afternoon and which she'd forgotten to put in her room. The desire to do a little waltzing left her abruptly. Instead she experienced a significant sinking of the spirit. Nick was not a topic of discussion that would brighten the rest of the evening and add to the romantic atmosphere.

"Those are very good pictures," Sam commented. His tone was even, but she sensed a sudden tension in the air.

"Yes," she said, sitting down on the sofa, wondering how to rescue the situation.

"Did Nick take them?" he asked, not looking at her. His gaze was fixed on the photo in his hand, a shot of her laughing, hair flying.

She nodded. "Yes."

He picked up another picture and studied it. "He knows you well, to capture you like that."

"I don't think I'm all that hard to know, Sam," she said slowly, aware of a sudden vague feeling of despondency. She willed it to go away.

He put the photos down and looked up, giving her a crooked smile. "No. It's usually all out there, right on your face, in your body language, in your words."

"Must be boring for a man who enjoys challenges, to have it all spelled out for you like that." She didn't know where that thought had come from, but there it was.

"Your openness is part of that irresistible charm of yours, Kim." There was a softness in his tone that she had not heard for a while, and a dark turbulence in his eyes that made her throat ache. She swallowed, looking away from him. Irresistible? She hadn't felt very irresistible where he was concerned. Quite the opposite.

She came to her feet, feeling uneasy, wishing Siti would come with the coffee, which she did promptly. She moved quietly and discreetly into the room and deposited the tray on the coffee table with a smile. Kim scooped up the photos, slid them into the large envelope they'd come in and dropped them on a side table out of harm's way.

Siti glided out of the room. Kim sat down again and picked up her cup. "You need to tell me exactly how you like your coffee," she said, changing the subject. "Then I can teach Siti."

"This is excellent," he said.

A while later Siti appeared in the doorway and announced that she was finished for the day and was going home unless there was something else they wanted her to do. There was nothing and they thanked her and wished her *selamat malam.*

It occurred to Kim that it had been quite a while since she and Sam had spent an evening alone together and she was aware of a tension between them. It hung in the air, growing more intense even as their conversation ambled on casually. She caught him looking at the envelope with the photos and felt her heart stumble in her chest.

She closed her eyes, took a deep breath and opened them again. "Sam, I'm not having an affair with Nick, as you seem to assume."

He gave her a dark, unreadable look.

"Nick is a good friend," she went on. "I like him, but that's all it is." She held up her left hand. The diamond in her ring sparkled in the light. "He thinks I'm married to you." Not, she thought, that that would necessarily keep people from having affairs.

For a long, pregnant moment, he just stared at her. "You've not told him?" he asked finally.

"No." She crossed her arms in front of her chest, as if protecting herself. From what, she didn't know. "I haven't told anyone," she added truthfully. "Not even Maya."

He gazed at her intently. "You're not exactly a secretive person. It must not have been easy for you."

She shrugged, not knowing what to say. It was true, it hadn't been so easy, although it had seemed such a harmless, innocent game in the beginning. She slipped out of the chair, feeling too restless to sit still. Standing in front of the big window, she glanced up at the night sky, clear and bright with stars.

"Kim?" He was standing next to her. "Would you rather not go on with it?"

Her heart thumped uneasily. "Go on with what?"

"With the pretense. Would you rather just tell people we're not married?"

"It wouldn't serve any purpose right now."

He searched her face. "Are you sure?"

She nodded. His face was so close, his body so near. Her heart pounded so hard. She couldn't bear the tension, the electricity sparking between them. It had been there all evening, undercurrents of wanting and longing.

He touched her hair, stroking a couple of stray curls away from her face. "You must be tired," he said gently. "You've had a long day."

Here was her opportunity to escape. If she wanted to. She didn't.

"I'm not tired, Sam," she said softly, meeting his eyes.

She saw the struggle in him, the hesitation, and then his mouth came down on hers, hot, urgent; a kiss, full of hunger and passion, flooding her with heat and desire.

He held her close against him and she wanted to melt into him, drown in the heat of him.

Then he let go of her abruptly.

"Sam," she whispered, trembling.

"I'm sorry," he said roughly. "I shouldn't have."

She swallowed desperately. "Sam, what's wrong?"

"Nothing is…wrong," he said with difficulty. He closed his eyes briefly. "We'd better not make this more complicated. Let's keep it simple, Kim."

Her heart turned over. "It is simple, Sam."

He gave a sad little smile and shook his head. "No, it's not Kim. Making love is, yes, but not any of the rest."

"I don't understand."

"It wouldn't be fair to you," he said, dark shadows in his eyes.

"Why?" She felt a flutter of fear at the edge of her consciousness.

"I can't make you happy, Kim," he said huskily, dragging out the words. "Not for the long haul."

Her stomach churned. "Sam, the long haul will have to take care of itself," she said recklessly.

He raked his hand through his hair. "It's better to be realistic and be honest about what's ahead." She noticed his hands, clenching into fists by his side, felt again the whisper of fear.

"I can't predict the future, Sam, but I know what I feel now and how I feel about you, and…and I'm not going to analyze it and take the magic out of it."

"Magic?" He gave a crooked smile.

"Yes." She smiled tremulously. "And I feel very partial toward magic. It's lovely stuff, Sam."

He didn't reply and she couldn't read his face.

"Sam, don't you want me?" she whispered.

Torment flashed in his eyes. "Oh, God, yes. I want you, Kim. I want you terribly, but—"

"I want you, too, Sam." She leaned closer into him, stood on tiptoe and put her mouth on his. "Kiss me," she whispered against his lips, wanting only to be loved, to have him close. "Please kiss me, Sam."

He made a tortured sound, something in between a laugh and a moan and hauled her fiercely against him.

And then he was kissing her, deeply, hungrily, and it was as if all the misery of the last few weeks evaporated in the passion of that kiss; as if they were together again as before, loving each other, needing each other.

They were in his bed, bodies entwined, eager, breathless, hungry for each other. Her body sang under his touch and she made soft noises, feverish with need.

It was wild and tempestuous lovemaking, unleashing a storm of unrevealed emotions. She lost all sense of time, of place, was only aware of Sam, the taste and feel and scent of him, the sensations more intense than ever before. Her body throbbed, arched against him in primal response as he urged her on with the heat of wild and erotic love play. She loved him and he belonged with her, in her heart, in her body. She was his, all his, and he was hers, all hers, moving together in ancient rhythms.

And when the storm had run its course and their love-damp bodies had stilled, they huddled close, not speaking, not wanting to break the spell.

He was watching her when she awoke. She smiled lazily and nestled into his embrace. "Mmm, Sam, you were a tiger."

He held her against him, saying nothing, and from somewhere a whisper of uneasiness again teased her mind. She raised her face to look at him.

"Is something wrong, Sam?"

He shook his head, shaking off whatever it was. He kissed her softly on the mouth and got out of bed.

"Would you like me to bring you a cup of coffee before you get up?" he asked.

"Mmm, that would be great."

She watched him as he pulled on a black silk robe and left the room. Nothing was wrong. Everything was wonderfully perfect.

With a contented sigh, she closed her eyes and remembered the night of loving, while outside birds chirped in the trees, a joyful sound celebrating the new morning.

It was a happy day. Kim puttered around the house as if she were a new bride in her new house, thinking how wonderful it would be to be really married to Sam. But there was no hurry. Right now everything was perfect.

Sam was home for dinner and they were spooning away the last bites of dessert when the bell rang.

"I'll get it," said Kim, and went to answer the door, finding Maya and Joel, bearing a gigantic cake and behind them more of her friends—the next door neighbors, Nick's parents, even James, all carrying wrapped packages as well as an assortment of plastic shopping bags. All beaming at her.

"Surprise!" they chanted.

Kim was too stunned to say a word, as was Siti who had appeared from the kitchen to answer the door.

"Happy birthday to you!" Maya sang, and gently nudged her aside so she could enter the house. The rest of the gang followed suit, singing loud and off-key. They traipsed into the kitchen and deposited the cake, the bags and the packages on the table and counter. Momentarily idle, they all grinned at her, delighted with themselves and their mission of human kindness.

"My birthday isn't until Monday," said Kim, having found her voice.

"And today is Friday," announced Maya, as if this

was news. "It was the best day for all of us to get this organized, except for Nick—he's in Surabaya, working, poor man."

"We have cake, champagne and music," stated James. "Let's party."

A veritable rush of activity ensued, punctuated with laughter. Everyone was in a festive mood, ready for fun and cheer.

Kim was overcome with this display of friendship, and wondered what Sam would think of this invasion of his house. They had obviously not expected him to be home from New York yet. He made his presence known the next moment, appearing in the doorway, surveying the scene, his expression one of amused surprise.

"Sam, old man!" James boomed. "Didn't know you were back."

"How are you, James," Sam returned.

"I am fine, fine," said James. "Cold champagne, beautiful women, what more can a man want?"

"A million dollars," someone suggested dryly.

Mrs. Harrison, Nick's mother, resorted to the social graces and asked politely if Sam minded if they had a party for his wife, adding that they would have included him in the planning if only they'd known he would be home and able to participate.

Sam, ever gallant, bade everyone welcome, and the party moved into the living room.

They sang, they ate cake, they offered her their gifts. They made embarrassing, sugary speeches about what a wonderful person she was, what a gift it was to them all to have her as a friend. They offered toasts, wishing her a long and healthy life, much prosperity, many children and eternal youth. Music filled the air, passionate and exuberant, and they danced. Everybody was having a wonderful time.

Sam played the gracious host, mingled and made conversation and when not dancing with Kim, kept watching her.

She was acutely aware of him, his eyes, the fact that he was observing her as she talked, danced, laughed with her friends, opened their presents, wacky, imaginative gifts—a jolly, big-bellied wooden Buddha, a colorful sarong they made her wrap around herself and show off, a pair of silver earrings depicting a wild-looking mythical creature and an assortment of other little gifts that she would treasure forever.

Finally everyone left and the noise-filled house was once again serene and quiet. Kim let out a long sigh and laughed. "I didn't know they were going to do that," she said to Sam. She was quite happy with the whole event; it made her feel loved and appreciated, which wasn't a half-bad way to feel.

Sam smiled back at her. "That's why it's called a surprise party, I believe. It was very nice of them, Kim."

"Yes, yes, it was." She glanced around the room. No damage had been done, thank goodness, not even during the rather exuberant dancing. No lamps or glasses broken, no food or drink spilled.

"You do have a talent for making friends, Kim."

She laughed. "People are everywhere. It's easy."

He didn't say anything to that, just kept smiling at her, with something in his eyes that unnerved her.

"What are you thinking?" she asked.

"That you're beautiful, all flushed and happy. That you're a special person and it's not hard to see why people like you."

Her heart fluttered excitedly. She wanted to reach out and touch him, she wanted him to kiss her, to make love. She wanted more than anything to tell him that she loved him, but deep down inside her, fear held her back.

Fear. Why was she afraid?

He put his arms around her and kissed her, his mouth warm and seductive. "Let's go to bed," he whispered.

It was a wonderful week that followed. She spent her days working on some of her art projects, going to a painting class and making arrangements for Sam's party. Kim loved living in the house, running the household and sharing her bed with Sam.

She tried not to worry about the small dark moments, when she knew Sam had withdrawn and wasn't talking. When she was aware of hidden emotions and thoughts. He was attentive and loving, made her feel as if she was the only woman on the planet. He swept her off her feet, made wonderful love to her and she couldn't imagine ever tiring of him, of ever wanting anyone else. Her job was almost finished, but she didn't want to go back to New York. She wanted to stay here with Sam.

But Sam did not mention the subject, never mentioned her return to New York, never asked her about her plans.

If only she knew what was bothering him. She could see it in his eyes, feel the tension in the very air around him.

Sam watched Kim arrange branches of purple bougainvillea in a large vase. She'd tied her hair back in a scarlet scrunchy, but a wayward curl had escaped and softly bounced against her cheek with every move she made. She was humming happily and his gut twisted painfully.

She was living a fairy tale, blissfully unaware that it could never have a happy ending. How could she not know? How could she not see?

And here he was, allowing her the fairy-tale illusion. He was a rotten excuse of a man. A selfish swine.

They were having quite a social life and Kim enjoyed herself. Coming home one night after a rather lively party at Maya's house, she felt happy and not at all tired. She put a Strauss CD on and began to waltz through the living room. "Come on, dance with me," she said to Sam.

He crossed the room, but instead of taking her in his arms, he picked her up and carried her out of the room.

"Sam!" she protested, laughing, pretending to struggle.

He carried her to the bedroom, set her on her feet and without a word began to kiss her and take off her clothes at the same time, fast and without seduction. His own clothes followed, ending up in a heap on the floor. There was a strange frenzy about him, a passion that seemed almost desperate as he began making love to her. Her body responded to his need, and she lost herself in the loving. She tangled her hands in his hair, caressed his strong, smooth back, feeling the tension in him. His face lay against her breasts and he moaned softly, whispering something she couldn't quite make out, something familiar, yet not...

"I didn't hear what you said," she whispered. "What was it?"

He lifted his face and looked at her with love-dazed eyes. "You feel so good, so soft and warm..." He lowered his mouth to her breast, taking in her nipple and teasing it with his tongue. Sweet torture, setting off ripples of sensation through her blood, emptying her mind of thought. Her body felt luscious and full, her breasts swollen with his touch.

His loving was full of dark intensity, and she gave herself up to him, to the urgency of his body, finding an answering fire rushing through her, finding release in a fiery explosion that left them both breathless and sated.

She fell asleep snuggled against his chest, his embrace tight, as if he were afraid she was going to leave him in the night.

The next morning she awoke, finding him awake and watching her. Before he smiled, she caught the sadness in his eyes and her heart lurched painfully.

"Sam?" she whispered.

He kissed her softly on the lips. "Yes?"

"What's wrong, Sam? Please talk to me."

He rolled away from her and lay on his back, staring up at the ceiling. "I feel like a miserable excuse of a man," he said lightly, but with just enough seriousness that she didn't laugh.

"How's that?"

"Because I want you to stay here with me after the party and not go back to New York."

"I don't have to go back to New York," she said, her heart thundering, her mind filled with sudden dread.

He stroked her hair. "Yes, you do, Kim." There was such immutable conviction in his voice, it rendered her momentarily speechless.

"Why?" It was merely a whisper.

"Because you're going to get hurt if you don't, and it will be my fault."

Her heart slammed against her ribs. "Why would I get hurt, Sam?"

"I'm a selfish bastard, Kim. I want you...I want you with me, but..."

"But what?"

"There's no future in it, Kim." There was despair in his voice. He got out of bed, as if he could no longer be close to her. Wrapping his black robe around him, he looked down at her. "You know that, Kim. You've said it yourself." His voice sounded strangled.

"I was wrong!" Tears burned behind her eyes.

"No, you were right." He closed his eyes briefly. "And I can't go on this way, pretending I don't know, no matter how much I want you. It's not fair to you."

How caring for her welfare he was! She suddenly felt

icy cold, her fear and despair now joined by a dose of rage.

She sat up in bed, pulling the sheet to cover her bare breasts. "You mean," she said, her voice trembling, "you mean that you want me and you'll have an affair with me, but you're not planning ever to...to have me be a real part of your life."

He turned his back on her. Shoulders hunched, he stood in front of the window and didn't answer.

She clenched her hands into fists. "Answer me!" she demanded. She wanted to hear it straight, clear, honest, no matter how much it would hurt. She needed to know. "Are you planning to ever ask me to marry you?"

CHAPTER TWELVE

FOR a moment he stood very still, his back rigid, his legs braced to the floor. Holding her breath she watched him, hearing with some other part of her consciousness the carefree chirping of the birds in the garden, seeing the sun shimmering its cheerful light into the room. Then he turned slowly and looked at her, his eyes impenetrable, unreadable.

"No, Kim, I am not."

There she had it, straight and clear.

Something inside her dissolved, drained out of her as if it were blood. She thought for a moment she would die, right there in the bed where they'd made love the night before, but her heart kept on beating. It seemed as if someone else was taking over, as if she wasn't really there in her body, in her mind, as if it all happened from behind a glass window.

"Well," she heard herself say, "thank you for telling me." And then she got out of bed, put on her kimono and walked barefoot out of the room and out of the house through the sun-drenched garden to the house next door.

She sat in Nick's mother's living room silent with shock while Mrs. Harrison brought her a cup of coffee and then, finally, she broke down with huge shuddering sobs and cried her heart out.

The party was in full, joyous swing and Kim surveyed the festive room and the people milling around, eating and laughing and having a good time. She had outdone herself. The house looked beautiful and welcoming.

Delicious food was laid out with artistry and flair. The music in the background added just the right atmosphere.

How she had managed to live through the past few days, she didn't know. She'd moved on automatic pilot, doing what needed to be done for the party, trying desperately not to think about Sam. She'd hardly seen him, although he had attempted to talk to her, saying he had never meant to hurt her, but she wanted nothing from him, certainly not meaningless words and empty gestures. She felt frozen inside.

She had fought against the impulse to pack her bags and leave that same day, but pride kept her from it. She had come for a job and she was going to finish it. She glanced around. And now it was finished and she could leave. Sam had his home, his own furniture, an efficient staff and there was no longer any need for her to stay. He did not need a pretend wife any longer; she could go back to New York, to her loft and her waiting friends.

She'd have to hang on till the end of the week, not having been able to get plane reservations for New York until then. She would stay with Maya and Joel, away from this house.

She found Sam standing next to her unexpectedly and her body stiffened involuntarily.

"You've done a magnificent job, Kim," he said quietly.

"That's what you paid me to do." Her tone was curt. She felt herself begin to tremble. She had to get away from him; she just couldn't be near him. She swung around and left him standing alone, by the big painting she had chosen. Blindly rushing ahead, she bumped into Nick, who had been invited along with his parents.

"I'd like to talk to you," he said in a low note. "How about outside, in the yard?"

"Sure." She followed him out the double doors. Lights had been placed in several locations, giving a fairy-tale atmosphere to the garden. Several of the guests had taken to the outdoors and she heard their laughter floating on the night breeze.

Nick led her to a quiet place in a far corner. "I don't want to be overheard," he said.

She hadn't seen much of Nick in the past couple of weeks. He'd been at home at the computer writing his article. He was leaving Indonesia the next day, flying to Singapore and starting a six-week tour of Malaysia and Thailand with a rented van.

The air was warm and fragrant with the scent of jasmine. Music drifted from the house, wafting around them.

Nick turned to face her. "I want to ask you something, and if I'm way out of line, please tell me."

"All right."

"My mother told me what happened two days ago, when you came over to the house."

Kim said nothing. She'd not told his mother the whole story. She'd sobbed that Sam did not love her, that she couldn't stay and was leaving.

"Are you planning to go back to New York?" asked Nick.

"Yes, I am." She felt emotionally drained and physically worn-out. She didn't really want to talk about this, not even with Nick who had been a good friend to her.

"I'm not asking for any explanations, Kim. You don't owe me any, but I'm sorry to know you're not happy."

"I'll be all right," she said bravely, touched by his concern.

"I worry about you, Kim."

She smiled in spite of herself. "Don't, Nick. I won't jump off a bridge or throw myself in front of a train. I haven't seen Paris in the springtime yet."

He laughed softly. "Kim, you are irrepressible, that's

what I like about you.'' He took her hand. ''You know I'm leaving for Singapore tomorrow.''

''Yes, I know.''

''I'd like you to think about coming with me on this trip. It will give you a chance to see some more of the Far East, and we'll have a good time.''

She didn't know what she had expected, but his suggestion took her by surprise.

''It…it sounds wonderful, Nick.''

''Here.'' He fished something out of his pocket and put it in her hand. ''This is a ticket to Singapore, same flight I'm on tomorrow. If you don't want to use it, throw it away, I'll understand.''

She sighed. ''Oh, Nick, I don't know…'' It was a tempting offer, but maybe it would be more sensible to go back to New York right away. Then again, being sensible had never been her strong point.

''You don't have to answer me now. Think about it, and I'll see you at the airport tomorrow if you decide to come with me.'' He put his arms around her and hugged her hard. ''This is not goodbye, you know,'' he said. ''If you don't come with me on this trip, I'll see you in New York.''

He released her, turned abruptly and disappeared into the darkness, not back to the party, but in the direction of his parents' house.

After a sleepless night, Kim packed her things the next morning, wrote Sam a short note, thanking him politely for the job and, feeling numb and exhausted, departed for the airport.

CHAPTER THIRTEEN

KIM glanced in the mirror one last time before opening her door to Nick. The room was small; the big tourist hotels had not yet made it to this tiny island, but it didn't matter to Kim. Not much seemed to matter to her anymore, although she made an effort putting up a happy front for Nick.

He looked cool in his white chinos and sky blue shirt, his hair still damp from the shower.

"Hungry?" he asked.

"Mmm, yes."

"You look beautiful, Kim." Nick closed the door behind him and advanced into the room.

She was wearing a long, slim skirt and a short silk top and was feeling quite a bit better than an hour ago when she'd arrived back at the hotel in shorts and T-shirt, hot and sweaty and tired. She'd enjoyed her tour of the lush tropical island, but a shower and clean clothes had much refreshed her.

"Thank you, sir," she said lightly, and smiled at him. "I can't find my purse." She glanced around the room, frowning.

Nick fished it off the floor behind a chair. "Here." He handed it to her, looking into her eyes, his hands reaching out and touching her hair. "Lovely wild hair," he said softly.

Her heart lurched at the tone of his voice, the look of love in his eyes. *Oh, no,* she thought. *Oh, no.*

"Kim..." he whispered, and his hands slipped down her hair, her shoulders. Then he took her in his arms and held her close against him.

Heart hammering, she stood rooted to the floor as his mouth closed over hers, kissing her softly yet with ill-concealed restraint. She felt the warmth and strength of his body against hers. She felt the love in his kiss and her heart began to hurt.

How could she not have known? How could she have been so blind?

Nick was a wonderful guy, a good man, a true friend. He was handsome and sexy and there wasn't a reason in the world why she shouldn't love him.

Only she didn't.

It was as simple as that.

She drew away from him. "I'm sorry," she said softly, "I can't." Tears of helplessness swam in her eyes. "I'm sorry, Nick, I'm so sorry."

"So am I."

Her heart contracted at the pain in his eyes. He did not deserve this. She should have paid more attention. What was it with her and men? Why couldn't she ever get it right?

"I didn't mean—"

He silenced her with a finger on her lips. "It's all right, Kim. It's not your fault. I did a very foolish thing, inviting you to come with me, knowing how I feel about you."

"I should have known," she said miserably. Looking back now, it seemed incredible that she'd been so oblivious. All the signs had been there. Why hadn't she seen them?

"I think your attention was elsewhere," Nick said, his mouth curved in a rueful little smile.

Was that it? She'd been so consumed with her own feelings for Sam that she'd been blind and numb to what was going on with Nick.

She swallowed the constriction in her throat, wishing with all her heart that she'd never agreed to come with him on this trip, wishing there was something to say that didn't sound like a platitude. There wasn't.

"I didn't mean to hurt you, Nick."

"I know, Kim, I know." He ran a hand through his damp hair, and his eyes clouded over. "Let's forget it," he said curtly. "Let's have dinner."

There was anger in his voice, and she saw the tightness in the way he held his shoulders, the steeliness of his jaw.

"You're mad at me," she said miserably.

"No, I'm not." He squeezed her hand briefly, a gesture of reassurance. "I'm mad as hell at that worthless husband of yours. I would cheerfully wring his neck, but since I'm quite sure you're still hopelessly in love with the man, I don't think it would increase your affections for me." He opened the door. "Come on, let's eat."

"Anything for me?" Kim asked the hotel receptionist, a beautiful Thai girl who was busy putting messages and mail into the boxes for the various rooms. Kim didn't know why she asked. Nobody knew she was here. Still, she asked every time she passed by the reception desk.

She had been on her own for the afternoon and had spent it reading a spy novel sitting on the beach in the shade of a coconut palm. Reading, and trying not to think about Sam. Nick had gone out to do a couple of interviews for the article he was writing, but was probably back already, she thought, glancing at the clock on the wall above the desk.

The girl shook her head. "Nothing," she said smiling. "But there's something for Mr. Harrison. Would you mind giving it to him? He's been waiting for this, I think," she added, handing Kim a large envelope. "And here are a couple of other things."

Kim reached for the small bundle of papers. Her fingers missed a sheet of paper and it fluttered to the floor.

She bent to retrieve it, seeing the red stamp at the top reading Faxed with the date filled in below it. To: Sam Rasheed, she read, the boldly handwritten words jumping up at her. Her heart twisted painfully at seeing the familiar name, then surprise filled her. Nick had sent Sam a fax, a hastily composed one by the looks of the big, untidy scrawl on the paper.

If you're sure you don't want your wife, I'm sure as hell going to go after her with all I've got. I've been my most moral self until now, but there's a limit to my patience. You must be out of your mind not to know what you are losing. She desperately loves you and is deeply miserable and she still wears that goddamned rock you gave her on her finger—why, God only knows. We'll be on this island for a few more days, at the address above, so you'd better make up your mind fast and come and get her.

Kim had read the angry missive before she could stop herself. She sank into a creaky rattan chair in the hotel lobby, her heart beating frantically, her breath trapped in her throat. She shouldn't have read the letter, of course; it was invasion of privacy, but here it was. More sins to feel guilty about, she thought wryly. I'm a liar and now I read other people's private mail. Where will it end?

She didn't know what to think about Nick's letter, whether she should be angry with him for interfering in her life, or touched by his generosity. What would Sam think when he read it? She couldn't begin to imagine it!

Having gathered a few shreds of composure, she made her way to Nick's room, across the hall from her own, and knocked on the door.

"Hi," he said, obviously pleased to see her. "Come on in."

She shook her head. "Maybe later." She wiped her damp hair away from her face. "I'm all sandy and sticky and I need to shower. I'm just bringing your mail. The girl at the desk asked me to give it to you."

"Thanks." He took it from her. "I'll see you for dinner then?"

"Sure. How were your interviews?"

He laughed. "An experience of sorts. I'll tell you about it over dinner."

Kim went to her room, grateful that the two of them had managed to keep things friendly between them.

She got rid of her sandy clothes, had a shower, dressed and watched world news on CNN. Tragedy all over the world and it barely registered. All she could think of was Nick's fax, sent earlier today, and what Sam was doing right now.

It wasn't so different from other times; she thought of Sam constantly.

It had been three days since Kim had discovered the fax, and still Sam had not come. The warm sea breeze played with her hair and stroked her face as she strolled along the sea on the hard, wet sand at the water's edge. The sun was setting, streaking the sky in soft pastels. She wished she could enjoy it; she wished she didn't feel like crying.

Nick had taken her on another tour of the island today. They'd visited some exotic temples and savored a spicy lunch in a restaurant by the sea. She was not hungry for dinner. She wanted to be alone, to not have to make conversation with Nick, to not have to be nice. It was not like her. She usually enjoyed the company of others; she enjoyed being with Nick and hearing his stories.

Well, she wasn't herself.

For the past three days she'd been haunted by the question of whether Sam would come for her. And if he did, what would she do? What would she say? But Sam hadn't been there when they'd returned to the hotel, not yesterday, not today.

Maybe he hadn't been in the office and hadn't yet read the fax, she thought, inventing reasons other than the one that made sense the most: He wasn't coming because he had made up his mind about their relationship and he did not intend to marry her.

She wished she had never read the fax. She wished she were back in New York so she could pick up her life again and pretend this whole ill-conceived adventure had never taken place. Pretend it had been just a nightmare and that now it was over.

Tomorrow she'd check with the airlines. When she got home she'd have a big party for her friends, something elaborate and fun, with good food and happy music for dancing. She'd need a theme. *A Life-Goes-On Party,* or some such thing. After all, life would go on, and she'd have to make something out of it.

Just thinking of it sucked the energy out of her. She sagged onto the sand and buried her face in her hands. I can't stand this, she thought. I can't stand being this way, feeling this way. It's so depressing.

She listened to the sound of the waves. It had a soothing effect. After a while she lifted her face. The beach was deserted. One tiny orange sliver of sun lingered on the horizon, then slipped away. It was quiet apart from the rushing of the sea.

She struggled to her feet, brushed the sand off her legs and shorts and turned back into the direction of the hotel.

In the distance two figures were coming toward her, a man with a child, it looked like, tiny little doll figures. A father and son, maybe, or a daughter. It was hard to tell from so far away.

She glanced down at her bare feet, kept watching them as they made step after step on the dark, wet sand, moving ahead almost trancelike, the sound of the waves oddly hypnotic.

Next time she looked up she saw the boy run across the beach toward the street, and the man, alone now, coming closer in the failing light.

Sam, she thought, I wish it were Sam. He looked like Sam—the same body build, the same wide shoulders. She felt her heart begin to beat a little faster. Maybe it was Sam. But in the dusky light it was difficult to really see.

She quickened her step, peering hard into the gathering darkness, hoping, wishing. She imagined herself running toward him, as you'd see in the movies, running with hair flying, and then throwing herself into his outstretched arms, crying, laughing. Her heart ached with longing. ''You came!'' she'd call out. ''You came to get me!''

And then he was close enough and she knew it wasn't Sam at all, just a tall, broad-shouldered stranger who strolled past her with merely a nod of his head in greeting.

The disappointment washed over her like a mountainous wave, leaving her weak, her legs trembling. You're an idiot, she said to herself. You've got to stop doing this or you'll go nuts. She saw Sam everywhere, heard his voice everywhere. Only it was never real. It was just her overactive imagination, the desperate longing of her heart playing tricks on her.

She trudged on, forcing herself to put one foot in front of the other, blinking away the tears that burned her eyes.

Sam wasn't going to come. She was never going to see him again. Yet every time she saw a tall, dark man she'd think it was him, and slowly, little by little, she'd go stark-raving mad.

The hotel should be close now. She peered into the

darkness, searching the beach for the entrance to the hotel grounds, a vine-covered portico guarded by an elab-
orately carved and decorated spirit house. Every morning
and night, the hotel staff put offerings in the little house
to keep the spirits happy—bits of brightly colored rice
cakes, flowers, pieces of fruit.

Out of nowhere, a tall dark shape loomed in front of
her.

"Kim?" said the dark figure.

Sam's voice.

Real. So real.

Panic surged through her. She turned away, afraid of
her own mind, her own delusions. She began to run,
away from the hotel, her heart pounding.

"Kim!"

He was coming after her. She could hear him behind
her, feel the vibrations of his feet on the ground.

"Kim! It's me, Sam!"

A moment of sanity. She stopped running and then
she felt arms around her, felt her face against a hard,
familiar chest.

"I'm sorry," he said. "I didn't mean to scare you."

No figment of her imagination, this. His arms were
real, his voice was real.

The pounding of her heart was real.

And the fiery mixture of her emotions—relief, fury.

Blazing fury. How dare he! How dare he cause her
all this anguish? She wrenched herself out of his arms,
glared at him in the darkness. "Don't touch me!" she
said fiercely, flailing her wrists at his chest. He inter-
cepted them easily, his hands grasping hers hard.

"Kim, listen to me!" His voice was calm and com-
manding and she revolted against it automatically, instinctively.

"Let me go!" She twisted her arms to no avail. His

hands were like vises around her wrists. He drew her closer, his face inches away from hers.

"Never."

A single word, said with so much power, it took her breath away. She felt the fight drain out of her, felt hot tears drip down her cheeks. Her body went limp and she sagged against him, against the hard, solid wall of his chest. His hands relaxed, pulling her down into the sand. He wrapped his arms around her, rocking her like a child. "I'm sorry," he muttered, "I'm sorry."

She closed her eyes, dragging in air, fighting against the tears. He was silent, just sat there holding her against him.

Her breathing calmed down. *I'm not dreaming,* she thought. Her cheek lay against his chest. She smelled the clean, warm scent of him, intimate and familiar. She heard the solid beating of his heart.

"I happened to see the fax Nick sent you," she whispered at last. "I didn't think you were going to come."

"I didn't see it until this morning. I was in Jakarta for a few days."

And he had come right away.

"How did you know to find me on the beach?"

"Nick told me. I saw him at the hotel."

She was silent, thinking of Nick, of him trying to help her in spite of his own feelings for her.

"Nick is in love with you," Sam said.

"I know."

In the dark he searched for her left hand, found the ring. "You never told him we were not really married," he said finally.

"No." She had been tempted to, yet in the end she had not been able to tell him the truth. She hadn't wanted to examine the reason, yet deep in her heart she knew. By telling Nick the secret she would have had to admit to herself that there was no more hope for her and

Sam, that they would never be a real pair, never belong together. And Sam knew why she hadn't told Nick.

His left hand trailed through her hair. "These last two weeks without you were hell," he said, his voice low and ragged at the edges. "Everything in the house reminded me of you." He spoke with painful difficulty. "I couldn't get you out of my mind, yet I kept telling myself it would have been selfish to have asked you to stay, that I had done the right thing by you to let you go." He paused for a moment. "The fact that you had gone off with Nick only seemed to prove it," he added huskily.

Kim swallowed but said nothing, afraid to interrupt.

"And then I got Nick's fax," Sam went on, "and I started doubting the wisdom of my reasoning. I began to think that maybe there was hope, and I remembered your saying something about magic and that you weren't going to analyze it."

She listened to him, breathing soundlessly, her eyes closed, afraid to say anything that would make him stop and crawl back inside himself.

He stroked her hair absently as he talked. "And of course I analyze everything and I try to be logical and rational, and—" he paused for a moment "—and I rationalized the magic right out of it all."

She could tell how hard it was for him to say what he was saying. She wished she could make it easier for him, but didn't know how. Shifting in the sand, she nestled closer against him.

"It was a terrible thing to do, Kim, because the magic was that you loved me, and it was what I wanted more than anything else in the world. I wanted a home with you, a happy place, like your family's. But I convinced myself that I wasn't the right man for you, that you would be happier with someone else."

But I don't love someone else, she said silently. His

hand was buried beneath her hair, lying warm against the back of her neck.

"All these years I never found what I was looking for in a woman."

"What were you looking for?" she whispered, peering up into his face in the moon-shadowed darkness.

"I never really knew. It always eluded me, until a few months ago, when I saw you again in New York. It sort of hit me over the head, even though at first I tried to deny it, rationalize it.

"It occurred to me that I had always loved you, even when you were just a kid. You were so open and funny and vivacious, all the things that I found irresistible. And then when I saw you again in New York, you were still that same person, except that now you were a woman and that changed everything. I fell hopelessly in love with you. I knew you were what I had always been looking for, someone who could draw me out of myself, someone who could make me laugh."

"Why then didn't you want to marry me?" she whispered, again feeling the pain of his rejection.

"Because I didn't think I could make you happy, and the thought terrified me more than losing you."

Her heart ached for him and the terrible loneliness he must have felt thinking he had to give her up for her own sake. Tears flooded her eyes. "Oh, Sam," she whispered. "Why? Why did you think that?"

"I would see you with your friends, who were all so different than I am, people who were like you, more open, easier to know, and I just knew that I wasn't the right person for you to spend your life with."

"I'm not in love with any of my friends, Sam," she said fervently. "I didn't fall for James, I'm not in love with Nick." She swallowed hard, and looked at the faint, dark shapes of her sandy feet. "Sam, I love you. I just do. Maybe it makes no sense, but I can't help feeling what I feel. I like feeling what I feel for you. It's wonderful. It's good."

"I've made you unhappy," he said bleakly.

"Only when you shut me out. When you wouldn't talk to me. When you didn't trust me enough to tell me your worries and problems."

"I'll have to learn," he said huskily. He tightened his arms around her and she could barely breathe. "I'm trying, Kim. I'm talking to you now."

"Yes." She felt a lightness bubbling up inside her, effervescent like champagne. It filled her with a joyous hope. She drew away from him a little to look up into his face. "I'll help you, I'll teach you!" The words spilled out of her. "I'll make you! As long as you promise me one thing."

"To honor and obey you?" he said dryly.

She laughed. "No. I mean yes, that too. What I mean is that you have to promise me you'll try, to be willing."

"I'm willing," he said. "For you, Kim, I'll do anything."

"Anything?" She sighed and then a chuckle escaped her. "That sounds really, really good, Sam. Do you know how dangerous a promise that is?"

"Yes, and I'll take that risk." He took her face between his hands and kissed her. "I love you. I want you in my life. I need you. I want to make you happy."

"I love you, too," she said. "Let's make each other happy."

"Will you marry me? Tomorrow, here on the island?"

She laughed softly. "Yes, if you're really, really sure."

"I've always been sure."

"You just weren't sure that I knew what was good for me." She slipped her hand under his T-shirt to feel the warmth of his strong, muscled back. "That's pretty arrogant thinking, you know. Implying I don't know what I want, that I can't decide what or who makes me happy."

"I'm a flawed man," he said dryly.

"I'm glad you realize that," she said with feigned hauteur. "I, of course, am perfect. Apart from the minor sin of telling lies to dozens of people about my being married to you."

"And you lied so very well."

She moaned softly. "I guess I am even more flawed than you are."

"I think we're about even." His mouth captured hers with a sudden fiery passion that set her body instantly aflame. All thoughts left her mind, except one—that she loved him and that he loved her. And that he had come to get her back, just like in the movies.

In the middle of the night, Kim woke up in Sam's arms in his hotel room on the other side of the island. Savoring his nearness, she lay still, listening to the whispering of palm trees outside his window, the rushing of the waves on the beach. The sea breeze floated through the open window and caressed her face, her bare skin.

A soft, languorous sigh escaped her and she felt Sam's body stirring against hers, his hands searching for her, finding her breasts.

She opened her eyes, trying to see Sam's face. Through the palm fronds, the moonlight filtered in, merely a silvery dusting of light across the bed. Reaching up she touched his hair. She could not see his face.

His hands caressed her, his mouth feathered across hers, tantalizing, teasing. In the darkness there was only touch and scent and sound.

"Bahibik," he whispered, a mere breath of sound against her cheek. "I love you."

And then she knew. It was the word her secret lover had whispered in her dreams. The word Sam had whispered that night of desperate loving. *Bahibik.* I love you, in Arabic.

She smiled, her mouth against the warmth of his neck. She felt happier than she'd ever felt before. With her hands she touched his familiar face, traced his mouth with her fingers.

"Who are you?" she whispered against his mouth.

She could feel him smile. "You know who I am, Kimmy, you know."

The world's bestselling romance series.

HARLEQUIN®
Presents

Seduction and Passion Guaranteed!

THE PRINCESS BRIDES

For duty, for money…for passion!

Discover a thrilling new trilogy from a rising star of Harlequin
Presents®, Jane Porter!

Meet the Royals…

Chantal, Nicolette and Joelle are members of the blue-blooded
Ducasse family. Step inside their sophisticated and glamorous
world and watch as these beautiful princesses find they have
to marry three international playboys—for duty, for money…
and definitely for passion!

Don't miss

THE SULTAN'S BOUGHT BRIDE (#2418)
September 2004

THE GREEK'S ROYAL MISTRESS (#2424)
October 2004

THE ITALIAN'S VIRGIN PRINCESS (#2430)
November 2004

**Pick up a Harlequin Presents® novel and you will enter a world
of spine-tingling passion and provocative, tantalizing romance!**

Available wherever Harlequin books are sold.

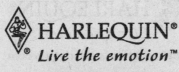

HARLEQUIN®
Live the emotion™

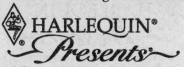

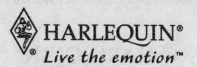

The world's bestselling romance series.

HARLEQUIN®
Presents

Seduction and Passion Guaranteed!

Your dream ticket to the vacation of a lifetime!

Why not relax and allow Harlequin Presents® to whisk you away
to stunning international locations with our new miniseries…

*Where irresistible men and sophisticated women
surrender to seduction under the golden sun.*

**Don't miss this opportunity to experience glamorous
lifestyles and exotic settings in:**

This Month:
MISTRESS OF CONVENIENCE
by Penny Jordan
on sale August 2004, #2409

Coming Next Month:
IN THE ITALIAN'S BED
by Anne Mather
on sale September 2004, #2416

Don't Miss!
THE MISTRESS WIFE
by Lynne Graham
on sale November 2004, #2428

FOREIGN AFFAIRS… A world full of passion!

Pick up a Harlequin Presents® novel and you will enter a world
of spine-tingling passion and provocative, tantalizing romance!

Available wherever Harlequin books are sold.

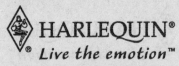

HARLEQUIN®
Live the emotion™

www.eHarlequin.com

HPFAUPD

Harlequin Romance®

A compelling miniseries from Harlequin Romance

Contract Brides

From paper marriage...to wedded bliss?

A wedding dilemma:

What should a sexy, successful bachelor do if he's too busy making millions to find a wife, or finds the perfect woman and just has to strike a bridal bargain...?

The perfect proposal:

The solution? For better, for worse, these grooms in a hurry have decided to sign, seal and deliver the ultimate marriage contract...to buy a bride!

Don't miss the latest CONTRACT BRIDES story coming next month by emotional author Barbara McMahon.

Her captivating style and believable characters will leave your romance senses tingling!

September—Marriage in Name Only (HR #3813)

Starting in September,
Harlequin Romance has a fresh new look!

Available wherever Harlequin books are sold.

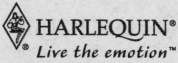

HARLEQUIN®
Live the emotion™

The world's bestselling romance series.

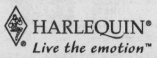